TABLE OF CONTENTS

CHAPTER ONE
GUM

"Claude! Look at what you've done!" Sabrina literally shouted, while trying to pull the sticky gum out of her hair, which, of course, turned out to be a futile effort.

"So?" Claude huffed with some guilt in his voice, but also excessive frustration. He did not want to "surrender" to a quarrel with a girl, because that would be immensely embarrassing by his stubborn boy's evaluation.

Five minutes earlier, Claude was still chewing his gum, which he should not be doing, and watching the clock tick. He was wondering when class was going to end. Biology, it seemed, was quite tedious to both Sabrina and Claude. Sabrina drew doodles of her friend Rachel in her book, and annoyed herself when she broke two pencils and couldn't get them sharpened. She grunted. Ms. Meryl glanced their way, saw the two uninterested red-haired popsicles, and continued talking. Well, she just couldn't do anything to get Sabrina's poor Biology grades up a little, and now she'd given up, or she would have frustrated herself like an angry cat.

Anyway, Claude was playing finger games across the classroom with his friend Henry (another horrid Biology devil). Claude blew a bubble with his gum, and as it popped it landed right in Sabrina's hair. At first, Sabrina didn't notice until she felt the sharp pain from the back of her head. She turned back to see Claude frantically trying to pull off something pink and sticky in her hair. Sabrina didn't yet know what happened when Claude, trying to help, basically pulled a handful of red hair from her head. So, as a result, Sabrina swiped Claude in the face seven times. Then she practically broke her voice yelling at him. That attracted the headmistress, until Ms. Meryl explained it away by claiming it was "audible fear from the children because of the ugly worm sample we had for our lab."

Ms. Meryl cleared her voice, staring at the two clowns with an ice-cold look that gave them shivers. She was famous all around seventh grade for her terrifying stares, and some boys called them "The Ghosts." Amusingly, the phrase wasn't very exaggerated. Right now, it was obvious what Claude and Sabrina were headed towards.

"Detention starts after school, at 4 o'clock, in Room A413." Ms. Meryl commented with a slight bit of complacency in her voice. Oh, how Ms. Meryl loved patronizing her students! It was well-known over the whole grade, and all other grades, that Ms. Meryl was (usually) the nice "Biology Cat," for she was so gentle. However, if you happened to act in a way that she could rightfully seize your neck and bring you to detention, you would become her mouse.

The class bell rang. So that was that.

~   ~   ~

Sabrina's friends Rachel, Dara and Magaritte gathered after class. Rachel nudged Sabrina,and smiled a little. Dara nudged Sabrina too. Magaritte gave Sabrina's arm a little squeeze. All of them had devilish, teasing smiles on their faces. Dara waved her hand, but Rachel was visibly bursting with the question she was about to ask—her whole face was turning into a tomato! No matter how hard she tried to stop them, giggling noises still came out of her mouth, so Magaritte said it first.

"What does it feel like to have your crush turn into your enemy?" Magaritte gurgled through the question, she was so urgent.

Sabrina choked on the water she was sucking down.

"**What on EARTH?**" Sabrina stared at Magaritte now. Every shape of her face, her eyes, her mouth, was distorted into a big "**O**". Then she dramatically puffed out her hair, and ran her right hand through the thick masses of tangled red weeds, while waving her other hand.

"**HE ISN'T MY CRUSH!** Just because we've both got this ugly red hair doesn't mean he's my crush!" Sabrina explained, pulling fiercely at a knot in her strands of wavy, red hair. Then she sighed in that dramatic way she enjoyed, and pretended to be exasperated. Dara and Rachel turned their heads and looked at each other.

Rachel twisted her mouth a little, saying "I didn't **QUITE** get the same report when we teased her last time." Dara raised her thick eyebrows, a gesture she loved which the other three girls called "The DaraBrow." In this case, it meant "**THAT** is an understatement, because I am totally sure that the last time we asked her she said she absolutely adored his red hair, and if we say anything about it she is going to swipe us with hers."

Rachel giggled. Although she didn't quite understand what Dara was thinking, the whole expression on Dara's face was so cute. Magaritte, on the other hand, was still trying to question Sabrina. Finally, they both laughed at the goofiness of the whole event. They were all clear what Sabrina said– the **LAST** time, not this time though.

Sabrina stomped and laughed, but also said sincerely: "He certainly is not my crush now." Then her face retreated from the giggling at the thought of detention with Claude, that red-haired popsicle. Her face became a dark, gloomy cloud.

CHAPTER TWO
SHOUTING

Sabrina stared at Claude with such a terrifying, furious expression it could be comparable to Medusa's blinding stare. She was like a jaguar as she spoke between her teeth. For a second Claude even thought he saw the long sharp teeth about to eat him. He pondered, but only for a millisecond, about what Ms. Meryl would do in this case. He knew that Sabrina was afraid of Ms. Meryl. Suddenly his thoughts jumped in and he pointed at Sabrina.

He said in a so-Ms-Meryl-way that it surprised both of them: "No, that doesn't work, because I'm not part of your food chain. I'm the Apex Predator here." Obviously, his attack worked on Sabrina. She stumbled back, still hissing, but backing up nonetheless. Claude on the other hand, was trying desperately to fit himself into the cranny between two walls of the classroom so Sabrina wouldn't burn him to death. The only visible part of him was a yarn-like ball of red hair.

"Claude…..." Sabrina hissed like a snake.

The sound of heels echoed in the corridor. Ms Meryl was coming.

"I'll deal with you later," Sabrina whispered menacingly through her teeth.

Ms. Meryl walked in with such pride that you might have thought she won the Olympics. Indeed, it was rare to see Ms. Meryl taking students into detention when she was so "gentle" most of the time, not taking into account how she had a long tirade to herself when she forgot to put sugar into her coffee this morning.

Ms. Meryl stood by the front door of the classroom, leaning back on her heavy boots she wore for the day. She liked to always lean her focus towards the heel part of her shoes (ninety percent of the time high-heels) for it relaxed her straining ankles, but it made her seem very small suddenly, and hunched.

"Guys, I am really disappointed, especially with you, Sabrina," Ms. Meryl said in her high-pitched-pity-voice that said 'I am super glad that you must obey me, and now you will listen to my hour-long speech about rules of behavior.' Claude sighed and whispered to exactly nobody: "Here we go again."

After a mind-emptying wave of words that seemed to have deep meaning, but were actually useless, Sabrina and Claude were at their desks copying their 'wrongdoings.' Claude was obviously annoyed, and stabbed his pencil into his desk every time he finished writing down a 'wrong.' That only made Ms. Meryl even more delighted, as she had made two students super angry but still unable to revolt. The table that Claude was writing on, however, wasn't having such a good time.

Ms. Meryl's phone rang. Frantically, she picked it up. She hid the desperation her eyes held at the sight of the number, and left the two students on their own. The ring-tone was quite special.

Sabrina told herself to focus on writing her 'wrongs.' Faintly, the ringtone she heard from Ms. Meryl's phone played in her mind, the rhythmic but systemic beats drumming in her ears. It was one of the phone-ring system's ringtones, but it was a bit different from the usual ones she heard when receiving calls from her friends. It seemed more formal.

As the pencil moved slower and slower, she was getting drowsy. Before she knew it, she was asleep.

Sabrina didn't know how many hours passed, but by the time she opened her eyes again, the sun was setting and Claude was gone. She gasped when she saw her paper of '**WRONGS**': it was almost empty except for a thin line of 'I will never swipe classmates.'

Frustrated, she picked up her pencil again and started writing. Suddenly she froze.

She heard shouting.

Sabrina was flustered. Who would be in school at this point? Why were they shouting? And most importantly, who were they talking to?

Walking slowly and silently, Sabrina moved towards the source of the shouting. Yes, it was coming from the classroom next door. Peeking through a small hole in the wall, Sabrina saw a short-figured woman, phone in one hand, the other hand moving up and down. Still not very lucid from her unexpected nap, Sabrina rapidly searched through her brain. She knew this woman for sure. Of course! It was Ms. Meryl! How could she have not known?

"No, No, No! I will never accept your explanation!" Ms. Meryl yelled into the phone, her hand ruffling through her choppy blonde hair. Her hair was a failure when she tried to cut and dye it at the salon last week, and she had ended up with a total mess. "I will never let Hilton go, and **YOU** will find him, or I will make you!"

Sabrina shrugged with curiosity. Hmm. Maybe Hilton was some important person to Ms. Meryl, so she was shouting about him? Nevermind. Better not to interfere with other people's business. Sabrina fetched her school bag. All she wanted to do now was go home and have dinner.

CHAPTER THREE
BIOLOGY CLASS

"Uh, come on," Sabrina groaned, huffing through a loose strand of her red hair, "I **HATE** biology class! Especially if it's the last class of the day!"

Dara, walking by, choked with laughter. "Oh, Sabrina! You…look like an angry puffer fish!" Dara bantered with Sabrina while literally attempting to laugh herself to death. Then she choked on her own saliva, despite all of her sassiness.

"I **NEVER** laugh on Friday. I mean, it's going to be the weekend once you finish school, but you still have to go to **BIOLOGY!!**" Sabrina exclaimed. She was clearly irritated— not at Dara's laughing, but from the annoyance of biology.

Dara was sitting on the ground now. She was holding her stomach so it didn't pop from the tension of her laughing. "Your…hair!" Dara barely made out the words properly.

Sabrina was a little curious, but also frustrated again when she reminded herself of Biology——again, not frustrated with Dara, but with Biology. Sabrina ran all the way down the corridor to the bathroom mirror. When she saw her reflection, she broke out laughing dramatically– her hair was all standing up. The long curly waves stood stubbornly like a porcupine, detesting gravity's pull on them. The grumpy but slow headmistress, Mrs. Allison, whose office was upstairs, ran with Olympic speed to see what was happening. When she saw Sabrina, she yelped with laughter.

"Seriously, what are you doing, Sabrina?" Mrs. Allison asked. She didn't expect a reply. Sabrina froze right on the spot when she thought she was going to get in trouble, but sighed in relief when Mrs. Allison said, "Oh my… You look like a porcupine, girl…"

The bell rang for the last class of the day.

Well, Sabrina was going to **HAVE** to face Biology now.

~ ~ ~

"Boys and girls," Ms. Meryl cleared her voice with a very slight croak. "Today we are going to learn about the procession and mechanics of proteins and how they interact to form our DNA."

To Sabrina, who had failed six Biology quizzes in a row this semester, that sounded much more like: "Today I am going to use my ultra-weapon proteins to destroy you all and make you fail, so that I can decode your DNA! (Sinister laugh!)"

After what felt to Sabrina like a million hours of 'how to crack your own DNA', Ms. Meryl handed a worksheet to each student. She announced: "You will be working for the rest of the class with your desk mate. For Sabrina, that means the person next to you," and gave Sabrina a 'you-know-what-I'm-talking-about' look. Well, obviously, her desk mate was the always-chewing-gum-in-class Claude.

"I will pass out the exam results from last week." Ms. Meryl started to give out a stack of papers to each student. And with that, the whole class turned and started talking to their partners all at the same time. Sabrina hoped she had Rachel as her partner. However, she turned left only to find Claude trying to hide a test on which he had scored a "53" in his desk. He was scared his mom would run around the whole neighborhood again with a racket, trying to swat him as if he were a fly. Sabrina shrugged.

"Claude." Sabrina yawned a little, stretching on the "aude" sound, and Claude jerked his head her way. "You don't really have to hide that, um, if you don't want to, because you're still one point higher than my whole Biology average." Claude half-smiled, because he really wasn't sure if that was a good thing or bad thing. Just as he sighed with a little relief, Sabrina spoke again.

"But…" the word itself was so piercing it stabbed in Claude's ears, "If. I. Get. Stupid strawberry-flavored gum in my hair again…"

She pointed at Claude. "I will call your mother immediately."

Her test sheets came back. Unsurprisingly, Sabrina failed again. Having 49 as a test score would make anybody cry except for Sabrina. In fact, if she could, she would have yelped in delight and ran back home shouting, "**MOM! I IMPROVED 6 POINTS FROM LAST TIME!**" And she would have shouted it so loudly you would have heard it from the core of the Earth.

Sabrina stared blankly at her worksheet— which was, to her, the direct door to madness. All she could see were letters, a diagram of an Amazon tree frog, and her name all squiggly on top of the worksheet. In a desperate but futile search to find a partner to work with, she peeked right. Seats were assigned. Henry, another one of the Biology devils, should have been here, but Rachel was there instead. Sabrina's eyes lit up with delight.

"Rachel!" she whispered, "why are you sitting here?" Rachel couldn't hear Sabrina with all the voices around her, and frowned. Sabrina attempted again, this time in the loudest voice a 'whisper' could actually be. A boy in the back row giggled at that.

Rachel shook her head at Sabrina, "psst, S. You have to be quieter than that!"

Sabrina resisted, "Yeah, I know, but why are you sitting here?"

Rachel sighed, "Seriously? I spent a whole 10 dollars so I

could change seats with Henry to sit with you for 2 days!”

“You gave that guy 10 dollars?!” Sabrina huffed with frustration, not mentioning how Henry ‘accidentally’ dyed her hair in art class with purple paint last semester. She had to go to the salon, where even that annoying woman who was an expert at fixing hair-fails “tssk”ed at the situation, and groaned.

“I know, I know, dude, but now I can sit with you!” Rachel explained patiently.

Sabrina hissed again, “Henry…That guy…I am going to get **REVENGE** on him!”

Rachel stifled back a laugh. Indeed, sometimes Sabrina could be quite funny even if she didn't intend to be. Goofiness was built into her **DNA**, even if it was not yet recognized as a type of chromosome. It certainly should be, at least for Sabrina.

Sabrina, ripping off a small piece of her worksheet, drew a piggy on top of it and wrote an arrow saying “I will make Claude and Henry into bacon for what they have done.” Then she drew a red haired, crying face representing Claude and a golden-haired, thin-faced boy, for Henry was quite wispy and thin for someone in the hockey team. In fact, the other boys in the hockey team were big and burly, and would look like smashing someone to pieces when they narrowed their eyes at something that particularly unsatisfied them. Not Henry, though. He'd probably just whimper and slink back like a retreating spring. Hesitating a little, Sabrina then added two tiny people, with silly lines mimicking braids that stuck out of their hair, on the top left corner, representing Rachel and her, who were pointing at the two crying faces and laughing. Reaching down to pretend she was picking up her pencil, she dropped the note on the floor, and kicked it slowly to Rachel.

Rachel, knowing what it meant, bent down and did the same thing. She laughed silently to herself and replied with a smiling face on it and wrote "Awesome art, **ARTS**." Sabrina was really quite good at art, and it would be an understatement to say that she made up seventy percent of the school's art gallery every month! Her friends often called her "**ARTS**", as the acronym of the accurate description "Artistically Renowned Talented Sabrina."

Just when she decided to pass the note back to Sabrina, both of them raised their heads in horror to see Ms. Meryl standing right by their desks, wearing her terrifying "Ghost" stare. Ms. Meryl made another announcement.

"Sabrina, you really need to consider your behavior these days. First, you were fighting with classmates, then you were passing notes in class! I will have to tell your parents sooner or later. And Rachel, you won't get out of it either. The next time, you're going to detention. If you want to know where that is, you can ask Sabrina." Adding a tint of the playful sarcasm you only use with people you are friendly with, Ms. Meryl clacked her heels against the floor. Then, turning to face the whole class, Ms. Meryl faked a brief smile and made Sabrina's favorite announcement: "And class is over. You are all dismissed. Have a good weekend."

"Yippee!" Sabrina literally screamed as she jogged out of the classroom, her almost-empty school bag bobbing up and down.

Dara, Rachel, and Magaritte, who were walking together with her, all smiled, which was basically a cover-up for a hilarious joke. Rachel stooped down, picking something up, and handed it to Sabrina. "You forgot your Biology homework. Don't thank me for it. It's my pleasure." She stretched on the "my" sound, just to be annoying, and waved it when Sabrina, the grumpy faced red-haired porcupine, didn't take it.

CHAPTER FOUR
CASE DEVILS

Saturday, a relaxing day for all. Not exactly for Ms. Meryl though. She was dressed in her plain high heels and wearing her classic light make-up, and knocked lightly on the door of Sabrina's house. Sabrina's mother opened the door with her guest-greeting, a broad smile. It was, Ms. Meryl found, a bit embarrassing to be stepping inside a student's house, and it wouldn't have played out this way, with her changing her heels into fluffy guest slippers Sabrina's mother laid in front of her by the doorway. When she suggested a parent meeting "to discuss certain current issues that would be easily resolved," she meant it to be at her office at school, not at her student's home, certainly.

Well, there was a misunderstanding, and when they both figured out each other's actual meaning, Sabrina's mother heartily welcomed Ms. Meryl to directly come to their home to visit. When Ms. Meryl proposed certain safety issues that the school might be concerned of, Sabrina's mother directly assured her she needn't worry "considering the tiny area of the town we live in" and "the people that live here all know each other better than bees living in the same comb." A weird comparison, but reassuring anyway.

Energized by this message, Ms. Meryl filed a report to the school on the parent meeting and filled in the address Sabrina's mother provided her, in elegantly confident cursive writing. Despite a nosy double-check from Mrs. Allison, the caring but sometimes annoying headmistress, on the address she filled under the "Meeting Location" column, everything worked out well enough. The report was approved of and received the stamp from Student Services quickly enough.

Now, standing at the front door, Ms. Meryl felt it might be inappropriate in general to come to student's homes, but it would be even more inappropriate to decline this warm, stout woman in front of her.

"Welcome, Ms. Meryl!" Sabrina's mother gestured to Ms. Meryl to come in. This is going to get hard, Ms. Meryl suspected, for how was Ms. Meryl going to tell Sabrina's 49-point-test fact to the nice, amiable woman in front of her! She smiled and spoke in a barely audible whisper, "Good morning, Mrs. Alvarez." She saw now that Mrs. Alvarez had taut skin which was slightly tanned. She had high cheekbones and wore a large, warm smile. Her eyes were large and almond shaped, forming a beautiful rhombus shape as she squinted her eyes a little from her broad smile. Every part of her seemed to radiate the word "affable." She had red, fiery hair too, just like Sabrina, but her hair was a deeper color, like rich, red wine, while Sabrina's was a lighter, more orange color, like the different layers of the sun at dawn. Mrs. Alvarez was a short woman. Her limbs were muscly and she was, most likely, a fast sprinter before she took on the role of motherhood. Her face gave hints of a serious yet stable and safe personality, but for now it was the merriest and most welcome face there could possibly be without any unnatural stiffness. Ms. Meryl's anxiety and uneasiness at this unusually placed visit was washed away like an imaginary tide pushed away, leaving no mark as if it had never been here.

It was quite a colorful home at first glance, and with an inquisitive eye one could see many artistic details in the organizing of such a cozy little house, with soft cushions and stuffed objects placed in various corners, giving the whole environment a sort of soft, gentle coziness. Some antiques and old-fashioned furniture sat, listening quietly away, in the front of the living room, adding a sense of vintage smartness to the scene. Ms. Meryl, still putting on a professional-teacher smile, sat down on one of the Spanish-styled armchairs in the living room.

"Sabrina's behavior is getting a bit off-track these days. Over the past month I have been a bit concerned for her. Her behavior is increasingly impacting her attitude and even her grades."

As the two women carried on in the living room, Sabrina's room was filled with laughter and talking.

"Come get me if you can!" Magaritte jumped up and down.

"I'm coming after you!" Rachel, smiling and shouting, ran after Magaritte in circles.

"I haven't said go yet!" Sabrina, wearing a whistle around her neck. She was laughing, in the frenzy as well, but also a bit frustrated that they had not listened to her as attentive players listen to their referee.

Dara was in a state of speechlessness. Puffing and smiling with confusion, she covered her forehead and sighed, "Sometimes these seventh graders can just be so silly."

As the captain of the team, Dara attempted to organize the girls again. "Guys! Don't forget our purpose. We came here to organize the case, not play." The three other girls, still in a rowdy mood from the playing, nonetheless obediently listened to their captain. Dara was good-natured, but when she got serious, they listened to her.

Rachel, holding a stack of profiles, announced: "This meeting of the Case Devils is called to action!" This was the opening 'ceremony' they had every time the meeting was about to start. Though Sabrina found it a bit funny, she still cooperated.

The Case Devils are the four girls–Rachel, Magaritte, Sabrina, and Dara–and they are a band of crime solvers! They get involved with different cases and solve them. In fact, this is their first BIG case out of many, and they have lots to explore! They also solved minor cases like the Missing Pocketbook Case, the Purple Hair Case, the Cut-in-pieces Biology Worm Sample Case, the Redhead Crush-saving Case, the Red Hair Dyed Black Case, the Thrown-out Biology Homework and the Disappearing Biology Paper Case—the cases are almost always directed at Sabrina, as one might observe, for she hates Biology the most.

The first to speak was Dara, in a serious tone: "Margarite, please give us the details of the most recent case."

Margaritte opened her laptop, pressed a button on the news clip, and a blonde reporter in a suit that was obviously too small for his muscular torso began speaking. The girls started giggling a little at his clipped, shrill voice, high-pitched like a bird, which might have fit a thin, old man more than a burly man.

"Guys! You are so mean, you should be focused on the case instead of on the news presenter," Dara announced, but the girls heard the smile in her voice. They stiffened up a little anyway. They listened with such attention that Dara was a little surprised. She expressed this through an inquiringly arched eyebrow.

"A man known as Hilton disappeared February 17th, a rainy day. His last name is unknown. Blonde hair, about 6 feet tall, approximately 50 years old. A witness claims to have seen him going into Bob's Cinema, Theatre 04. Another witness was said to have seen him quarreling with a man about 40 years old."

The clip ended, and a momentary silence hung in the air as the girls sucked in air slowly, weighing the complexity of the seemingly unsolvable case. It was Dara who broke the silence first.

"Hmm. This is the most complicated one yet. Rachel, I want all the inhabitants in this town with the first name Hilton on your laptop. Sabrina, clarify who the two witnesses are. Find the exact claims they made in the report. See if you can also get their alibis. Use public footage from the city-wide system that we broke into last time we solved the Biology Paper Case. And Magaritte, search for security camera footage outside the theater, and hack into police cameras at red lights." Dara gave out the instructions while looking at the title of an old newspaper entry about a different case; the entry was posted about five years ago, and Dara frowned slightly as she compared the entry with the present case at hand. She clicked into the website and let out a frustrated smile at her own mistake: the entry was a report on a missing dog, even offering a $100 reward. Well, at least the dog had a nice name: Fortinbras. Anyways, it had nothing to do with the case, and Dara complained to herself a little for not focusing on the task at hand. She continued to rummage through the long list of websites reporting several different cases, scrolling down and reading the information quickly. The other girls, it seemed, were all working tenaciously too.

As they worked inside, Ms. Meryl prepared her bag to leave. The talk with Sabrina's mother went extraordinarily smoothly, and Sabrina's mother nodded at every point Ms. Meryl spoke about Sabrina's behavior. This valuable, kind understanding between teachers and parents can be rare. Many of the other parents she visited were either impassive or somewhat too protective of their children, causing them to not believe her about the details she told of their children's conditions at school. Acknowledging this positive influence, Ms. Meryl even gave Sabrina's mother some advice on how to incite an interest in Biology in Sabrina. Ms. Meryl gave Sabrina's mother materials she organized for Sabrina to be able to review at home.

A fierce round of laughter sounded again in Sabrina's room, loud enough to be heard clearly from the living room where Ms. Meryl sat. She could make out the bell-like sound of Sabrina's laughter and

Dara's hymn-like chuckle. A tiny squeal sounded, most likely from Rachel. A slightly French-accented shout aroused another round of giggling, supposedly Magaritte then, who was the only French girl within the group. So, there they were, the four besties together again: Sabrina, Rachel, Dara, and Magaritte.

"What are the four girls doing inside?" Ms. Meryl asked Sabrina's mother, curious.

Sabrina's mother could only let out a helpless shrug and chuckled.

"Oh, something to do with case-solving. The girls want to be detectives." Leaning in a little, she whispered, "almost all the cases they have solved have been about finding Sabrina's biology homework or her half-completed projects." Ms. Meryl laughed a little at this.

Sabrina's mother continued: "But Sabrina won't let me know what they're up to, says it's some tradition of the organization. They call themselves the Case Devils, and probably are working on a case with a missing man, the Hilton case." Ms. Meryl stiffened a little at the name Hilton. She nodded a little, though not wanting to probe more about the girl's self-organized group for fear of betraying more about her secret.

For a second the two women fell silent, listening to the endless chatter.

Ms. Meryl's phone rang.

She forgot to turn the volume low, and now the phone buzzed loudly. Both of them jumped at the robotic melody of the ringtone, more like a tedious screeching. It was the same ringtone Sabrina had heard when she was in detention. Ms. Meryl looked up in embarrassment, but the good thing was Sabrina's mother only gave her a nod and a smile. With that, Ms. Meryl picked up her phone quickly and pushed the door open to leave. No one, she hoped, had seen her glance at the number on her phone with such bitter contempt.

Inside the room, the four girls were replaying the news report again and again in a desperate attempt to figure out what had actually happened. Sabrina twitched. She had been born with an astounding sense of hearing and memory. When Ms. Meryl's phone buzzed with that ringtone, she flinched. Ignoring Dara's frown, Sabrina dashed out to the room when sounds spun across her mind. That ringtone. Ms. Meryl's shouting. But the one word that struck Sabrina was: Hilton. Was he the one from the case? Might he be a different person? Sabrina didn't know. But she wanted to. Ms. Meryl had shouted about Hilton. Ms. Meryl was unwed–she even specified that the large ring on her ring finger was for "a more aesthetic decoration because the lovely ring would only fit on her ring finger" on her self-introduction on the first day of school. She also didn't have children. That means…she might be related to the Hilton in the case. Now that the ringtone had sounded again, Sabrina grasped her chance to ask her.

Sabrina ran over to Ms. Meryl and stopped right in front of her. Ms. Meryl, concentrating on her phone, almost jumped when she saw Sabrina staring at her.

"Oh! Ah…" She seemed a bit shocked. Ms. Meryl tried to stuff her phone into her pocket. Sabrina, with her exceptional hearing, heard Ms. Meryl whisper into her phone, her teeth biting on every syllable: "I'll deal with all of you. But later." In her best effort to not be funny, Sabrina cleared her voice, and acted like she was some big detective.

"Ms. Meryl…" Ms. Meryl was backing away. A thin layer of sweat gathered on her make-up, and for a second she seemed a bit out-of-sorts. It was far from her usual, formal personality. Sabrina considered that she might be pushing a bit too much into other people's business now and suddenly wanted to ease the tension that came with Ms. Meryl's uneasy response a little. She added a silly pose–standing with her back bent forward and feet facing inwards so she looked like a superman–to the dialogue.

"Yes? Sabrina…What do you want to know?…um…" Ms. Meryl was obviously getting more stressed, and that only made Sabrina even more confident of her prediction. Despite Sabrina's attempt at settling the sudden uneasiness, Ms. Meryl seemed so stressed by the way Sabrina was looking at her that she took no notice of Sabrina's silly change in pose.

"Do you know something about Hilton?" Sabrina raised one eyebrow and squinted, a facial expression she and Dara both liked. Ms. Meryl was still denying it with her best effort, but her melting eyeshadow gave her away. "Oh, um... no, of course...um...not. I don't even know who he is." That phrase did it.

Sabrina might not have much evidence, but she didn't need any more. She was now almost certain of the truth in her prediction that Hilton had something to do with Ms. Meryl's conversations. After all, she had stammered and her sweating forehead caused her eyeshadow to melt. She was nervous when the conversation turned to Hilton.

Ms. Meryl, knowing that she had revealed too much, hurried away from Sabrina's house. She wanted to get out as fast as she could, but her high heels were an inconvenience. Instead she walked quickly on her tiptoes, trying to get away as quickly as possible. She couldn't keep her secret much longer. She wasn't even sure why she wanted to keep it a secret–the police weren't helping her anyway. Maybe she just didn't want to get anyone else involved. She wanted to do everything by herself. Even if it meant putting herself in danger. She did not want others in danger. Case Devils or not, she supposed, she was on her own.

~   ~   ~

Sabrina was giddy with excitement. She jogged back into her room, where the meeting was still going on. As she pushed the door open, it was obvious Dara was disappointed. The disappointment hung in the air, like a thick moisture sticking in Sabrina's throat, refusing to leave. Sabrina felt she had just gotten vital information for the Case. Dara, however, was not to be interrupted and understood the environment they were in. If any of their parents or classmates saw them, the Case Devil's meeting would have to be canceled. She glared at Sabrina cold-eyed like a snake.

"Sabrina," Dara lectured her, "you should not go outside in the middle of meetings because all this has to be top secret. TOP SECRET! You have violated the rules we set." For a moment Dara considered if she had been a bit too aggressive. But, thinking back to how Sabrina violated the organization's traditions, Dara decided to reinforce the rules once and for all. Her forcefulness quieting a little but not softening, Dara continued in her cold tone.

"We do not want other people interfering with our work, especially when this is our first official case. In addition, you just interrupted me and the video, so you owe an apology to the group." Sabrina knew better than to argue back, so she forced an unconvincing "sorry," and returned back to her seat.

Sometimes Dara thought maybe she shouldn't take these activities as seriously as she did now. Still, Dara was grateful for the opportunities she had these days to meet with friends, which were growing rarer and rarer as academic studies demanded much more attention than the preceding years. And what if one day they really broke an important case, whether by accident or intentionally? As far as she knew, all four of them wanted to be detectives in the future, working in forensic labs or as the leaders of police groups, as private detectives or as crime-scene analysts. Maybe it seemed a lofty dream now, but who knows if it would come true in the faraway future? That, she told herself, was why she should take these Case Devils meetings more seriously than before.

Now Dara wasn't in the mood to let her go. "Sabrina, please present us with the reports I assigned to you," Dara instructed with a cold sarcasm, though not in an extremely antagonizing way. Sabrina stared at her feet. She didn't have any reports to present, because when she should have been preparing the documents, she was outside dealing with Ms. Meryl.

A little bit embarrassed, she mumbled, "Um... I don't have any reports…" Staring at her feet, she felt her face burning, though it wasn't flushed.

Dara was clearly irritated, "Okay, then go back to your seat and stop wasting our time." Sabrina, a little bit annoyed at not being granted the chance to explain herself, sighed and sat down with relief.

Magaritte was discouraged and talking to exactly nobody, "We will never crack this, guys!"

This reminded Sabrina of the detail she found about Ms. Meryl, and she rushed out the words before she forgot them, "Guys, you know what? I think I've just found something very important!" Sabrina's eyes shone with delight.

Dara waved her hand impatiently, "What is it?"

"Well..." Sabrina cleared her voice like Ms. Meryl often did when starting to announce something. "Last week, I went to detention with Claude, and in that period, Ms. Meryl answered a phone call."

"So?" Dara said. "Does that have anything to do with what we are talking about today?" Dara rested her head on her knuckles, shrugged, and frowned at Sabrina.

"Well, let me finish first." Sabrina didn't bother to explain much, but went on with her story. "The phone call Ms. Meryl answered had a ringtone that played a distinct melody. Later, I heard Ms. Meryl shouting at her phone when she stepped out during detention, and I heard her say something about Hilton. Both of the phone calls Ms. Meryl received had the same ringtones. They must be from identical sources. Which, I now assume from her nervousness, should be related to the very case we are talking about now. The Hilton Is Missing Case.

Dara's emerald-colored eyes betrayed no sign of emotion except for a sliver of light, a spark of excitement that escaped the window to the soul, lighting her eyes up a little.

"And then what? Go on, Sabrina!" Dara urged.

Sabrina raised her head a little with pride.

"When I dashed out of the meeting today," Sabrina nodded slightly at Dara as she explained what happened, "I questioned Ms. Meryl to see if she knew Hilton. Then, in her phone call she seemed utterly frantic, even a bit miserable."

Rachel cut in.

"Hey, but what was it like? You know, Ms. Meryl was supposed to be serious like she was the WHOLE time." Sabrina thought for a second before replying.

"Um...she just looked very weak, as if she was about to collapse the next second. And you know what? She was even staggering when I asked her! Normally, she might have sent me to detention again just for stepping in her way if she was grumpy." Sabrina made a little face of disdain, and the three others nodded in agreement while smiling at the memory of how Sabrina did often get into trouble with Ms. Meryl. Not serious trouble, of course, more like a teasing way.

"Anyway," Sabrina continued, "the last detail that made me sure of my prediction was the way she backed away from me today. I think she knew that she had exposed a secret, and scampered away."

Magaritte, who was a little confused, said: "So what was your final conclusion?"

Sabrina answered in her 'serious' tone: "My conclusion is that Ms. Meryl knows Hilton, and might be one of his family members. Or, at least, definitely is involved with him somehow and is worried. Whomever she is contacting on the other side of that phone call definitely isn't helping her much, or is annoying her so much she has to shout at them "

At this point, Rachel, who was concentrating on her computer just then, hit the table and stood up so loudly Dara jumped.

"Oops." Rachel was a little embarrassed. "Sorry, guys, I didn't mean to scare you. I was just a little too excited about my findings."

Sabrina looked up at that: "Say it, Rachel!"

"Well...I was just looking up what Dara assigned me, and look what I've found!" Showing her screen to everybody, Rachel was grinning from ear to ear. "There are only 2 inhabitants in this town with the first name Hilton. And guess what? One of them is named Hilton Meryl! He is also 52 years old, which fits into the category of 'approximately 50' as the news reporter claims."

Dara was also smiling a bit, but she still mentioned, "What about the other person?"

Rachel almost laughed out loud at that, "Oh Dara, the other one is only a 4-year-old kid!"

The four girls cheered.

CHAPTER FIVE
MEANWHILE...

The dark figure seemed as menacing as ever in the weak light of the basement. Holding a knife in his hand, he suddenly waved it at the chair in frustration. The other figure, tied to the chair, screamed desperately, toppled over, and felt a whip of wind as the knife slid just by his nose. A threat. The ropes that bound him to the chair cut painfully into his flesh, but The Man, whose shadow had been darkened by the dim light, took no notice. Then The Man in a frenzy cut off a strand of his own dark hair. He was on the brink of insanity.

"This is what will happen to you..." he hissed. The dark figure gestured as he pretended to slit his throat with his knife, "for all you've done! You deserve such consequences, you devouring monster, who consumed every single drop of my mother's blood!"

Waving his knife around, his teeth bit on every syllable. The person tied to the chair shifted uncomfortably, unable to sit up again.

Though his mouth was covered, he still tried to mumble faintly, "Well, I didn't know that." The dark figure turned abruptly, and there was a dazzling reflection from the knife.

"Excuse me? I don't care what you know. Don't plead for mercy later." The dark figure threw the knife down. Thud. The clatter of the metal blade. The scraping of the blade on the rough cement. Toppled over, the person on the chair was getting dizzy. Irregular blood flow was blurring his vision. His eyelids were getting heavier. All he remembered seeing was the dark figure inching towards him. Then his eyes closed.

CHAPTER SIX
THE QUARREL

The Case Devils decided to meet again at Sabrina's house the next weekend. Sabrina was giddy with excitement. She had already prepared all sorts of files about past cases across the US. She had profiles of the criminals and who solved the case, just so that Dara could see she was actually working hard. As the doorbell rang, Sabrina was bringing in all sorts of different juices the girls would like.

Dara entered the house, and the two other girls followed her inside. Seeing the files on the table, Dara frowned a little.

"Um... " Dara said. Sabrina was confused, and she felt her heart weighed down a little. "I don't think we need all that today, Sabrina." Dara continued, "We're going over the incident you had with Ms. Meryl last week. "

Sabrina was upset.

"Then what did I do all this for? Wasting my own time just so that you can ignore my findings?" Sabrina, suddenly angry at exactly nobody, but mostly herself, stood up instantly, and started yelling and ripping papers. The three other girls were startled. "I organized and printed all the cases in the past decade related to disappearances, reported on by multiple news sites."

Dara was a bit perplexed, and attempted to calm Sabrina down, "Oh, um, well, you don't have to be... um... so angry. I mean, we can still use it, if that's what you want." Dara said quickly, a little guilty.

This just provoked Sabrina further.

"What do you mean? Like, I printed all this so I want you to use it? I printed this to actually help you, not just for you to use it so you won't hurt my feelings!" Sabrina was gasping, but also rapidly cooling down from her sudden emotional tantrum. She started to hiss out her words now, instead of speaking properly. A sudden cold rationality reached the usually jolly spirit, and she now spoke in a composed manner, not like her usual silly self. She realized what a fit she had been in just moments before, and now spoke with a settled, dignified arrogance. The girls were, in fact, quite astonished at this sudden transformation; Sabrina wasn't like her usual self anymore. This girl in front of them, with her frizzy red hair, freckled cheeks, and warmingly cute dimples when she smiled, seemed taken over by another side of her, the calculating, calmed-down mindset.

"Actually, after this mess," Sabrina pointed at the torn papers lying silently on the long desk of her cozy bedroom. She pursed her lips in some measured disgust, "and after the stupidly childish tirade that just happened," she let a dramatic pause hang in the air before going on as the girls all stared unblinkingly at her, "I am beginning to think that all my time spent on this meaningless association is an absolute waste." The girls all shuddered inwardly, a little, for the open conviction Sabrina had made echoed their thoughts a little, weakly, but enough to have an impact on them. They, too, started questioning the actual use of this club they assembled. But, gazing from one familiar face to another, they restrained themselves with the reassurance that this was their one moment to themselves, when true friends meet. Solving cases *was* fun, an undeniable fact for all of them. Their dreams, the girls told themselves, were in these cases. Although it took a lot of studying to become a private detective or police detective these days, they were willing to leap over the obstacles. It seemed that this momentum was waning for Sabrina–and rapidly.

Sabrina continued icily, with a sarcastic sigh: "Such a waste of time."

The girls hesitated. Rachel, worried about her, patted her lightly on the back and shot Dara a see-what-you-did look. Dara was consumed by guilt. She opened the door to leave. Magaritte, not wanting to be involved in any of this business, decided it was better to leave as well, and followed Dara out.

In the living room, Sabrina's mother saw Dara and Magaritte leaving, and gave them a confused glance.

"What's up, girls?" Sabrina's mother asked in her friendly Spanish accent.

"Nothing."

The door closed.

CHAPTER SEVEN
CONFLICT RESOLVED

It was a Monday as ordinary as any other. Sabrina readied her bag for school and took the sandwich her mother had prepared for her. The day was rainy. Gray clouds clustered together in the sky as if the whole world was crying. Staring drowsily at the droplets of water collecting on the bus window, Sabrina wondered for a moment, what was Dara doing now? Or what about Rachel? Resting her head on the cold glass, she floated into sleep.

The buzz from a mixture of talking, laughing and the beeping of cars woke Sabrina up. She had arrived at school. Now walking half-awake, her legs ached from having sat so long on the bus. She looked around for Rachel, but Rachel wasn't here. Surrounded by the crowd, Sabrina stood there helplessly. The people around her were collected into small clusters of friends, each talking and laughing. But without Rachel, Sabrina suddenly felt that she had gotten up on the wrong side of the bed. The sky felt extra gloomy, as if shrouding the world with mist and dark clouds.

Then she turned around and saw a familiar face. Dara. She looked moody too. Both Rachel and Magaritte hadn't come today, what an awkward coincidence. Absent on exactly the same day. Sabrina stared at Dara, and Dara stared back at her. For a moment a quick smile flashed across the desperate faces of those two people. Those lone figures seemed to have forgotten all the unpleasantness of the recent past. For a single moment Sabrina even had the urge to run over to Dara. But it was only just an instant. Realizing their conflict, Sabrina turned her head away. The rain dripped from her umbrella: drip, dap, pop. Dara, in reaction to Sabrina's walking away, also walked away. She did so with arrogance, without looking back. So the conflict wasn't really solved, after all.

~   ~   ~

Sabrina gazed out the window. Rain still poured down just like it had in the morning. Inside the classroom, everything suddenly seemed so cozy in contrast to the huge gales of wind blowing outside, as if the weather was enraged at nothing in particular. The math teacher, Mr. Cley, was a tall and skinny man. He wore wire-rim glasses, much like Dumbledore's in Harry Potter. The work he was teaching now was definitely most tedious. After surviving a hour-long lecture, Sabrina now had to endure completing a project with Claude–when both of them knew absolutely nothing about the topic. She heard the math teacher babbling about something to do with the Pythagorean Theorem. Sabrina's mind was elsewhere. Drifting in a kind of half-sleep, she was so bored that she started drooling. The drool spread out and reached the border of Claude's desk.

"Ewww!" Claude cried with that kind of shrill, baby voice boys have during their 'girls- are-eww' phase. Sabrina, not at all woken up, was still murmuring something about fried-chicken tenders, until she felt a sharp pain right in the center of her forehead.

"Sabrina Alvarezzz Fyre!" Her math teacher shouted in his deep, croaky voice. He had already thrown a small eraser at Sabrina without effect. Even though Sabrina sat in the second-to-last row, she could still feel the fiery rage burning right in front of her face, all red and hot. Waking all of a sudden, she was still a bit confused about what was happening. Until she realized she slept through the whole class and drool-trespassed on Claude's desk. Claude was still yammering with that shrill, childish voice. He pointed at her and tried to move his chair so he was as far from Sabrina as possible.

Around the classroom, all the student's heads were turned and looking at Sabrina and Claude. The students were rapt, as though this was some kind of dramatic play. Mr. Cley was glaring so ferociously that anyone who caught his eye might faint. Sabrina felt more miserable moment by moment. She was knotted up. She felt like she couldn't breathe properly. Her vision was starting to blur. Sabrina broke into tears. It was exactly like her behavior in the latest meeting in front of Dara.

Everything was muddled up like a big bowl of lumpy oatmeal. It was a mixture of blurred images bobbing up and down. Conversation buzzed all around, tears fell. Guarded by the three girls, Sabrina was escorted to the bathroom. The girls were on the lookout for anyone who looked at Sabrina with any hint of mockery or laughter. She could feel students from other classrooms curiously peering out to see what was going on. Before she knew it, she was standing before the mirror, gasping and panting. She felt hands on her shoulders. Her vision was starting to clear now, and she saw who it was—Dara! At the sight of her, Sabrina cried even harder.

"I'm… sorry...Dara..." Sabrina was gasping again now. Dara, standing by the side, was smiling.

"It's okay," Dara seemed comforting now. "Happens sometimes."

CHAPTER EIGHT
BREAKTHROUGHS

The Case Devils met again, attempting to go over a bigger breakthrough. It had already been a month since they started the investigation. Their case hadn't even gotten a single clue yet.

"Right, guys," Dara was her serious self again, "It has been a long time since there was a breakthrough, or even progress, on the case. Right now, we suspect that Ms. Meryl has a certain connection to Hilton. So..."

Sabrina bobbed in before Dara finished, "So we need to confirm his identity!"

"Exactly." Dara nodded in approval.

"Are we able to contact Ms. Meryl? She is the most vital primary source. At least for now." Rachel added.

"I think I know where she is!" Sabrina suddenly answered, "She just posted a new social media status update." As Sabrina demonstrated on her laptop, the three girls surrounded her, eager to see the message.

The post read: @Coffee_Cream_&_Cones is just **FANTASTIC**! Come try it.

It was posted with a photo of an iced latte piled with whipped cream.

"Let's go to Cream and Cones Coffee!" Sabrina said. The four girls instantly hopped on their bikes, put on their helmets, and off they went.

~   ~   ~

"Whoa!" Rachel got off her bike and gasped for air. "I never thought pedaling could be so **TIRING**."

"Me too," Dara agreed as she locked up her bike and took off her helmet, "If we just didn't pedal that fast we wouldn't be so tired."

"I want to walk next time!" Agreed Magaritte.

"Come on, guys." Sabrina was already opening the door. "Let's see if the horrifying Biology teacher is inside."

Dara chuckled to herself, "Looks like Sabrina is never really going to get along well with Biology."

The four girls went in.

They easily spotted Ms. Meryl in her bright pink dress and puffy jacket that was nevertheless fitted. She was listening to music with her headphones, and didn't see the girls until they were right in front of her.

"Oh! Hi girls." Ms. Meryl said. Today was her jolly persona, and she smiled at the four girls. "What are you here for? Do you have any questions from Biology class?" Though everyone was smiling, Dara could still feel Sabrina rolling her eyes.

"Ms. Meryl, we do have some questions for you. But in fact, they are irrelevant to Biology." Dara answered, in her serious tone, as usual.

Ms. Meryl was certainly starting to get nervous. Rachel noticed a thin layer of sweat starting to gather on her forehead, as if she was trying her best to hide a half-revealed secret. Dara sat down on the seat opposite Ms. Meryl and asked in that sort of "this-is-a-trap" way of interrogating:

"I believe that you heard about the case a week ago where a 50-year old man named Hilton mysteriously disappeared?" Dara raised one of her eyebrows.

Ms. Meryl was frantic now. "How do you know about it? HOW?" Ms. Meryl quit hiding her secret.

"Well..." Dara shot a look at Sabrina, "It all started when Sabrina went to detention with Claude for the first time."

Ms. Meryl looked puzzled, "But I thought she went home?!"

"No," Sabrina shook her head lightly and with a bit of guilt, "I was drowsy and slept the whole time. Then I heard someone shouting in the classroom next door, so I peeked through a hole in the wall and recognized you. Also, when you were preparing to leave after you came for a visit to talk to my parents, your phone rang. I recognized that ringtone immediately. It was the exact same ringtone as the one you answered in detention. This made me suspicious of who it was. When I got contacted about the Hilton case, I recalled you shouting to the phone at detention, saying something about 'Hilton,' though I couldn't remember the last part."

Rachel nodded in agreement, "Yep! We also looked up all the inhabitants present in this area and there were only two residents with the first name Hilton: one is a 4-year old child, but the other one is named Hilton Meryl. So that confirmed our suspicions."

Ms. Meryl, looking up in astonishment, lowered her voice and said, "Since you know it already, I'm not going to hide any more." She took out a small photo from her bag. There were 2 figures in it: one was Ms. Meryl, still a teenager, and the other was a man with features similar to her.

"This is my father," Ms. Meryl said. She talked in a slow and creepy way, as if in deep hatred of a specific individual, hidden behind the shadows of society, "He disappeared on February 17th."

"That guy is Hilton?" said Sabrina, surprised, a bit TOO loudly. Dara quickly covered her mouth. Fortunately, no one in the cafe looked up at them. Rachel sighed in relief.

"Yes," Ms. Meryl replied, her teeth biting on every single letter as if devouring the words themselves, "His name is Hilton." She stared at Sabrina with a coldness the girls had never seen from her before.

CHAPTER NINE
HILTON'S AMULET

Inside the classroom, Sabrina was as annoyed as ever. Staring out the window, she saw the sun shining down gently on the branches outside. A small bird chirped. Weird thoughts popped in and out of her mind. Hearing the bird's chirp, Sabrina suddenly got very mad, "Why don't birds have to go to school! They don't even have Biology class!"

Ms. Meryl, who clearly heard what Sabrina said, walked slowly towards her desk. Towering over her, she whispered, "Birds don't have to go to school, but they have to learn to fly. So close your tiny mouth and learn your Biology."

Though the day was bright with blazing sunlight, Sabrina felt as gloomy as ever. Tuesday was the day she hated most. It was crammed with all sorts of classes she didn't like: Math, Biology, Spanish, Physics, World History, etc. Even worse, the very first class of the day was Biology!

Sabrina, feeling so very unhappy, started stabbing her poor eraser with her pencil.

"Argh! Why do only humans have to go to school! I hate Tuesdays!" Sabrina was at the very peak of her frustration. Her inner-self was already bellowing. However, that didn't keep her from the unavoidable reality that she was sitting in the Biology classroom. She still had to listen to Ms. Meryl babble about genetic transformation.

Sabrina looked around, observing her classmates. Rachel didn't seem as optimistic in Biology as she normally would be. Dara was resting her head on her folded arms and staring at her feet, while Magaritte was trying her best NOT to fall asleep. It certainly wasn't the liveliest classroom in the world.

Ms. Meryl wasn't in a good mood either. She had left all the handouts she made for today's class at home, **AND** forgot to bring the flash drive with her PowerPoint presentations. She had to recreate her PowerPoints in a rush, and get the files ready for printing again.

It seemed that everyone was having a bad day, except the sun, which was still scorching and burning at this point.

~   ~   ~

Over the course of the day, Sabrina survived not only Biology, but also other ordeals. It rained during PE class, and they had to stay inside and do homework. In Math she was forced to work on a problem set with Claude.

Sabrina was still arguing with Claude over the Math assignment in the school bus headed home.

"I am *never* going to do all that work!" Claude shouted at her while Sabrina was getting off the bus. Sabrina, annoyed, turned back, rolled her eyes, and went home.

School had finally ended. Sabrina got home and went straight to her bedroom. She wanted to finish reading her novel so she could work on her English project. The book was boring, but the project was due tomorrow. She was anxious and didn't have an idea of how to start it.

"Honey! Come and wash your hands for dinner." Her mother called from the kitchen.

"Oh, okay," Sabrina was so tired her lips didn't even want to move, the words rolled from her lips as more of a stressed sigh.

She ate her dinner silently, and from that face of hers, you could tell she was getting more frustrated by the minute.

Her cell phone, charging by the sofa, rang with an annoyingly loud 'Ding!', followed by a silly ringtone that Dara set for her number, an unusually out-of-character thing to do for serious, not-joking Dara. The ringtone did, actually, make Sabrina want to smile every time, for it played out tremendously and Sabrina dragged her feet to pick it up.

"Hi, this is Dara." Dara was on the other side of the telephone, and her voice sounded urgent.

"What's up?" Sabrina clearly wasn't in the mood for nonsense. She was in the mood to entertain exactly nobody.

"Can you schedule a case meeting now?" Dara asked, unaware of Sabrina's mood. It was evening, and since Dara had already finished her homework today, it seemed perfectly reasonable.

"Like, right now?"

"Of course! I asked Rachel and Magaritte and they're totally fine with it. By the way, Ms. Meryl is also coming."

"Wait, what?" A nervousness tensed in Sabrina and made her throat suddenly sound thick. It was not because of the feeling of proximity to Biology that Ms. Meryl brought with her, but because of the sheer weirdness of the fact that their teacher, usually considered so superior and impassively detached, was suddenly engaging in one of the girl's assemblies. It seemed very out of place indeed.

"Why is Ms. Meryl coming? Did she actually agree to do this? Like, literally? I mean, we used to work after-school Biology lessons for extra-credit right, but usually they were supposed to be held at school! Is she really coming with us? "

The four girls in the Case Devils did actually arrange weekly meetings with Ms. Meryl that she, despite all her busyness, seemed to be able to squeeze out precious time for. They worked on Biology tasks mostly, filling up Sabrina on some key concepts in review sessions that she might have forgotten or gotten confused with. Occasionally Ms. Meryl would teach them more advanced parts of Biology that the other three girls might be interested in, though Sabrina was no nearer in understanding these complex pieces of Biology knowledge than a penguin was nearer to flying.

The majority of the time it acted as a study hall, which actually felt nice and was working well. The girls were able to help each other and Ms. Meryl helped them too, not only on Biology, but on other subjects too that she herself managed in mastering when she was at the age of the girls. Even though her university degree was in Biology, she could, of course, also teach the girls some other concepts, for the studies, still at a middle-school level, were not difficult for her. She would also give them chances to do extra credit work, like creating a presentation or a Biology-based board game. She created an assortment of opportunities she would later open up to the whole class too, to be fair.

Sabrina took this time to really make sure she understood her content and practiced with Biology problems. She reviewed by doing projects, including posters and presentations. Despite Sabrina's clumsy Biology efforts, the art in her presentations was resplendently awesome. The other girls took time to finish schoolwork or delve into deeper academic studies, occasionally working on high-level Biology too. This time might not be mandatory for them, but they were all happy to keep Sabrina company. She was the center of the four girls, this vibrant, lively spirit that had become the pearl of the group, the jolly creation warming them up. These meetings usually happened twice a week and Ms. Meryl hosted them in a free meeting room at school.

Now, on the phone with Dara, the questions were rolling out of Sabrina's mouth quickly and unexpectedly, even surprising herself a little.

"Does Ms. Meryl know what we are going to discuss? Have you guys already made it clear to her that we are getting involved and have decided to help her with the case? Also, are Rachel and Magaritte okay with this sudden arrangement? And you, too, Dara, are your parents okay with this? I thought maybe there would be some problems with parental permission or issues of that sort."

Dara gave off her light-hearted chuckle again. She acknowledged Sabrina's sudden nervousness, and found continuous amusement in the way Sabrina questioned things. Sabrina relaxed a little at Dara's high-pitched laugh, for it almost always told of settled matters. Dara was such a good administrator and so adept at organizing events– Sabrina needn't worry. Something about Dara's tense leadership could be, well, sometimes annoying, but it was definitely reassuring and reliable. From the way that Dara was speaking now, Sabrina felt relieved, and she waited for Dara to explain how the issue of parental permission and Ms. Meryl's coming to an agreement was resolved.

"All our parents are totally fine with it. We told them that it would be just like the usual meetings we held with Ms. Meryl at school, just this time it would be at one of our houses. Also, the meeting room at school is actually occupied now by members of the administration, remember? Mrs. Allison announced that in assembly, so we told them that we had to make-do with hosting this activity at home. Ms. Meryl agreed too; we already explained our intentions and she accepted." Said Dara.

"Do you think we could host it at your house or at Rachel's?"

Dara spoke with her usual, self-composed eloquence that made it unbearable for people to refuse her offers. Sabrina worshipped that confident articulation. When she spoke, she stammered and an uncertainty seemed to creep over her. Her previously confirmed thoughts swayed again, increasing in their force: from a gentle rocking making her question herself a little, to a ferocious gale, striking her thoughts down.

"Of course! This is the first official case we've had. If we contribute a large part in solving it, we might get rewarded! And, well, it helps us practice our logic if we are going to be crime-solvers when we grow up. Um, well, sure! I'll see to it. Come to my house then." Sabrina ended the call and went downstairs to talk to her mother, who responded by singing a light-hearted Spanish tune, and set to work immediately to prepare things.

~   ~   ~

Knock-knock. Sabrina was waiting at the door, and her "crew" had finally arrived.

Dara announced: "This is a meeting of the Case Devils with Ms. Meryl."

Rachel bobbed in before anyone said anything, "The best way to progress now is to track Hilton's life FIRST. We want to know about Hilton and how he interacted with whomever is involved in his disappearance."

"We can go pick up Hilton's things." Ms. Meryl blurted out a little, unlike her usual peaceful self. But, it had been a most stressful time for her. One could obviously see the state she was in even from first glance–her hair was ruffled and so dry it was straw-like, and large, dark circles hung under her eyes. Her eyes dragged down although she wasn't drowsy, and suddenly she seemed aged, different from the young woman weeks ago with blonde, gold-like hair and rosy cheeks. Now she was grey and dull, as if the glow of liveliness had been rubbed out of her.

"What are we waiting for?" Sabrina was excited, "Let's go! Maybe we could get a drive to Hilton's house to check things out."

Ms. Meryl chuckled to herself, "I have never seen her so enthusiastic in Biology class." She pulled on her serious face quickly though. She said again with the same casual eloquence but a thicker tone, making her voice powerful: "No." She said it with such sudden fierceness that the girls were a little astonished. Her blue eyes glinted and that tranquil, ancient, yet powerful energy came back into her. "On second thought, no. It is not safe for you guys. Not at this point of day. I am okay with bringing you over to his house to collect any clues–I was, in fact, arranging that – but it must be during the day and with parental permission."

Dara stood up slowly at this. "Our parents were totally fine with this meeting."

Ms. Meryl countered, "But bringing you out to an unfamiliar place at night? Impossible." She waved her hands.

Dara declared again, "We will discuss it."

The four girls all huddled together to discuss a plan. Ms. Meryl was outside in the living room making small talk with Sabrina's mother.

"So, what now?" Magaritte asked mischievously.

"We call our parents and request their permission." Dara said lightly as she reached out and took her cell phone out of her pocket, as if it were the easiest thing in the world–which the girls knew, it was not. Dara's mother was really strict and sometimes, it seems, too protective. This bold action inspired the girls too and they also brought out their devices to ask for the "supreme" permission of their parents.

Rachel and Magaritte had all confirmed things with their parents, as long as they were safe and could be tracked using their phones or watches by their parents. Sabrina stepped downstairs and her always-agreeable mother immediately consented too as long as Sabrina was brought home before 10pm and kept in constant watch of Ms. Meryl–"for Sabrina is sometimes too curious and gets herself in trouble too often," her mother said with a laugh.

Dara was, in fact, the one who was challenged by dealing with her mother. Despite the volume on her phone being turned to the minimum, the cold voice with hidden tints of fierceness could still be heard on the other end–muffled, but not, in any way, reducing the unspoken tension that hung in the air. However, at last, she managed to persuade her mother. Dara assured her mother that she was "safe and sound" and was going to be home before 10 pm too. Her mother was not fully convinced, but consented nevertheless.

The girls cheered a little and that sparkle of merriment weaved its way back into their vivid souls. Dara too, seemed to cheer up more in her attempt to revive the other girls' spirits–which was more like an attempt to self-reassure. The grey, melancholic streak in her eyes was still there. It just faded a little.

Ms. Meryl shook her head a little while murmuring to herself, wearing a small smile of amusement on her face. Won over, Ms. Meryl could now only bring them to Hilton's house. The girls were eager to collect clues and nothing could stop the lively spirits as they hopped their way to the parking lot, where Ms. Meryl's car was parked.

~　　　~　　　~

"Okay guys, has everyone fastened your seatbelts?" Ms. Meryl said as she slid gracefully into her seat.

"Yep." The girls said by some weird coincidence, all at the same time, the excitement thick in their voices. They seemed to be sparkling with energy all of a sudden, even Sabrina, who was feeling worn out just hours ago when she first arrived home from school.

Ms. Meryl revved her car engine, and off they went. The drive felt long, even though it was only 20 minutes. It felt like a millennia. Rachel was getting a bit carsick and dizzy. All three girls were staring intensely at Sabrina, who brought her Nintendo Switch and was fiddling away at it. Clicking frantically on her screen to beat the Big Boss, she finally passed a level. Magaritte, forgetting that Ms. Meryl was concentrating on driving, cheered a big "Yay!" Ms. Meryl, scared, jumped off her seat and almost lost control of the steering wheel.

"Margaritte! That was so dangerous!" Ms. Meryl started lecturing. "I could have lost control and crashed!"

"Oh," Magaritte looked at her feet. "Sorry."

The car finally got off the highway and eventually pulled into the driveway before a large cottage.

Sabrina stared at the house in awe. "I love it here! I hope someday I can have such a big yard!"

"Me too." Rachel was pointing at the patio on the second floor. "That's just so amazing! I would grow grape vines all over it and it would be wonderful for afternoon tea!"

Ms. Meryl cleared her voice, "Guys." Sabrina looked up instantly and she suddenly thought it was Biology. Ms. Meryl often used this tone when criticizing people in Biology class, and Sabrina was one of the students that heard this version of Ms. Meryl most often.

"Don't forget what we're here for." Ms. Meryl continued as she looked at Sabrina and Magaritte, who were still admiring Hilton's house.

The tall door opened silently as Ms. Meryl pushed it and stepped in.

~   ~   ~

"Eeek." The door closed slowly behind them as Ms. Meryl was trying to find her way in the dark toward the switches that would light up the living room.

"It's so dark in here…" Rachel was starting to back up, falling into Sabrina.

"Wooo," Sabrina, still as childish as ever, pretended to be a ghost.

"Ahhhhhh!" Rachel screamed at the top of her lungs, which made Ms. Meryl, previously unaware of what was going on, jump right on her heels.

"Guys! What's wrong with you? Just turn on the lights!" Dara replied. She had just made an unsuccessful attempt to stifle a huge laugh that would no doubt ruin her reputation. "Well, Dara, you've just failed to hold back that laugh," Sabrina pointed out.

Ms. Meryl sighed.

"We need to track Hilton down first," Magaritte said.

Ms. Meryl now seemed to try to find something in a frantic manner. She was scuffling around the whole house like a mouse, and flipping things over.

"Where is it?!" She said to no one, as she tripped over a box of cookies on the ground.

"Come over here guys!" Sabrina suddenly shouted. She had already gone towards the second floor. "Look what I found!"

Hearing that, a sense of tension and excitement rose up in Ms. Meryl.

"Could that be the…" Ms. Meryl temporarily shook the thought out of her mind and climbed upstairs.

~   ~   ~

"Hmm…" Dara stared at the box, attempting to figure out what was in it.

"It appears to be a somewhat old box," Rachel stepped out, her face still a bit pale from Sabrina's prank.

At this time, Ms. Meryl appeared, still gasping for air from rushing up the stairs. "Wow…this is really it!" Ms. Meryl circled around the box, not believing it was really there.

The girls were confused.

"What is going on?" Dara probed Rachel a little as she whispered in her ear. Sabrina played with a tangle of her wavy red hair while staring at Magaritte with arched eyebrows.

"What is what and why?" How did Ms. Meryl recognize the safety deposit box? Sabrina's mind was crammed with a billion weird questions of all sorts, and was as confused as ever.

"What's going on?" Rachel inquired, while peeking at Dara to see if she knew.

"I don't know." Dara replied, putting on her most serious voice, still trying to reconstruct her just-shattered reputation.

"Well," Ms. Meryl said. She spoke without taking her eyes off the deposit box. She was still gulping in huge mouthfuls of air (due to the fact that she was so amazed she forgot to breathe). "The Meryl family has a treasure, passed down since our first generations."

Sabrina certainly didn't feel like she wanted all this suspense, and interrupted abruptly. "What is it, then? Don't tell me that the treasure is this old BOX down here." Sabrina giggled playfully, pointing at the box.

Ms. Meryl sighed and muttered: "Always so childish." Returning back to her topic, she started again, "There is an heirloom, an amulet carved from green emerald. It is said that it protects whoever is its master. And Hilton has been the guardian of this heirloom for years."

The four girls pushed in to see the contents of the box as Ms. Meryl kneeled down and, in a skilled and proficient manner, flipped the numbers in a whirl of motion no one saw clearly. She opened the box with a click.

Ms. Meryl's eyes widened with horror.

There was nothing in the box.

The room was suddenly dipped into silence, as if time itself had stopped to look at this matter.

Ms. Meryl fell backwards and almost blacked out from surprise. Magaritte and Dara caught her just in time. Ms. Meryl leaned on one side of a table in the middle of the room.

"What…" Ms. Meryl's voice trailed off and she just stood there, bewildered and not able to totally believe the amulet was gone. It hung in the air. The realization that Hilton had disobeyed a family rule and now the amulet was gone with him. The ancient heirloom preserved for years, was most likely broken or sold by the kidnapper.

"He was told not to wear it out…" Ms. Meryl was gabbering to herself. She cursed softly under her breath.

"What's the matter?" Sabrina stared innocently at Ms. Meryl.

"The amulet. It should have been inside the box. But it isn't, and Hilton must have worn it outside to show off to his friends again." Ms. Meryl spoke slowly, her voice raspy.

"Hilton violated a family rule. The master of the amulet shall not wear it, but must keep it in the box…" Ms. Meryl explained to Sabrina and the others.

"Oh. No, no, no. This is just ridiculous. How could he?" Ms. Meryl whispered to herself as she poked her head mindlessly around, staring at the open box.

"What's this?" Sabrina said as she poked around the deposit box and grabbed a small sheet of paper from the bottom.

Ms. Meryl leaned over and took a long look at the sheet of paper. It was written: **g@689hiltonc30481noejcodechhi3**

"Wait. Could it be…" Ms. Meryl suddenly dashed towards her computer and took out a small card from her pocket. "Let's see. Enter passcode." Everyone's focus was on the computer. It was suddenly so quiet they could have heard a mouse.

A new page came up on the computer.

"YES! It worked!" Ms. Meryl waved her arms in the air.

"What happened?" Sabrina was curious, but also confused.

Ms. Meryl cleared her voice (in the same way that made her famous).

"I always tried to log into Hilton's bank account. I desperately needed to check on his spending but I just couldn't get the code right. But this is the code!"

"So… You've basically made it into his account?" Rachel asked.

"Yes." Ms. Meryl was now scrolling down the page, her eyesfixed on the screen.

"Let's check his account then!" Dara was enthusiastic, and had obviously given up on retrieving her serious and stern reputation.

Ms. Meryl nodded and scrolled down the page.

What she saw stunned her.

CHAPTER TEN
IMPOSSIBLE SPENDING

Ms. Meryl was staring at Hilton's spending record intensely.

"No...This is...impossible..Certainly not...." The anxiety and concern leaked out of her face. It was suddenly very quiet.

"How could anyone do this? I mean, he piled up $20,000 dollars of debt in just a month!" Sabrina gasped.

"Guys, it's pretty late, and you are supposed to be home soon." Said Ms. Meryl. "I am going to give you each a copy of this information tomorrow. Dara, I want you to graph this chart. Rachel, find the average increase of spending per month. Sabrina, calculate the value of debt in total. And Magaritte, find the line of best fit in the total increase of his spendings."

"Ms. Meryl sounded so much like Dara when she spoke," Rachel observed to the other three girls. She was still a bit pale from Sabrina's prank, although some light, rosy color has returned to her usually flushed cheeks. Sabrina and Magaritte nodded in agreement while smiling at Dara.

"Sounded like me? What?" Dara echoed while pointing a dramatic finger at herself. The girls laughed a little before following Ms. Meryl out of the house.

~   ~   ~

Sabrina made herself focus on the events that were unfolding slowly. She tried to collect the clues and weave them together into a suitable story. But it was a jigsaw puzzle that fell out of place, or, rather, refused to fall in place. Think. Her mind wandered. Emptily she asked the air: "In what type of scenario do you suddenly start spending and collecting a pile of debts, but then abruptly stop?"

It was recess, and the girls were all assembled together in the equipment storeroom, an old wooden cabin loaded with all sorts of equipment–hula hoops, jump ropes, volleyballs, and so many more strangely shaped yet fun toys–that were mainly for the elementary-school kids, but which everyone enjoyed. It all gave an odd sense of coziness. There was the wooden smell of the old storage room, the neatly piled assortment of playground apparatus that sat quietly on the shelves or huddled tightly in their baskets, even the thin layer of dust that hung in the air. It all gave a sense of a secrecy the girls loved. Sabrina sat atop a large, dark-brown colored wooden case, which, following her curious exploration, revealed a dozen tennis balls. Magaritte half-leaned on a soft volleyball that almost ran out of air and was hung on the wall mercilessly, while Dara and Rachel each took a side on one of the stout, flat dressers.

"Well…" Magaritte answered. "Investors lose or gain money according to the stock market, don't they?"

"Then what kind of activity could provoke this?" Sabrina thought out loud.

Magaritte suddenly spoke as if an idea popped from her mind. "Gambling! You could become a millionaire in a night, or lose all your money and have a pile of debts."

"Yes, exactly!" Dara was waiting for this answer.

"Why didn't I think of that sooner!" Sabrina whispered to Magaritte.

Rachel nodded, as if considering something. "The only problem now is why didn't he spend ANY money in the last 2 months before he disappeared."

Sabrina suddenly popped in. "His disappearance might be connected to this, we just don't know how."

The girls fell silent again, unsure what to do next. They did predict that maybe Hilton gambled, but there were so many aspects of the case that they did not know. Aspects that they would have to work out. How he went missing. What actually happened. The thoughtful silence lingered in the room, reluctantly giving way to the sound of the world outside the wooden storeroom. Outside, the faint chatter of high school teenagers and the ear-piercing screams of playful kids seemed to increase in volume as the girls' focus on the hearing senses intensified. The unusual harmony the sound made was quite unexpected, though, and it freed their minds of the usual logic it automatically sunk into. The girls sucked in this eerie but soothing tranquility before the bell rang for the end-of-recess, scaring Dara, who was absorbed in thoughts of her own.

CHAPTER ELEVEN
EAVESDROPPER

"Ms. Meryl?" Dara was knocking on the door to Ms. Meryl's office.

The rusted, green hinges of the door in the old school creaked. The door opened slowly, as if taking its time.

Ms. Meryl stood behind the door with her classic smile. "Oh. Dara, it's very late now, and I wonder why you haven't gone home yet? Your parents will be waiting for you." She gestured to Dara to follow her into the office. It was already 5:30 in the evening, and most of the teachers had gone home.

"Well… I had to do my history project. But… anyway, I came here for a major breakthrough in the case." Dara sat herself down on one of the spinning chairs that were opposite Ms. Meryl.

"Oh, really?" Ms. Meryl's face lit up with hope.

"Yes." Dara lowered her voice. "The other three girls and I have decided that Hilton is very likely a gambler. And he's into it A LOT." Dara exaggerated that last word.

The sky was turning dark rapidly. There was a rich mix of velvet colors in the sky, putting on a grand show of crimson and violet. It was as if the clouds themselves were burning. The colors gracefully slid into each other like the dance of dragons. It was a diversity of hues moving with harmony and elegance. For a moment Ms. Meryl was entranced, staring out the window and admiring the last traces of daylight.

"Ms. Meryl?" Dara brought Ms. Meryl back to reality. The serenity of the moment before vanished into nothingness.

"Oh! Ah…what was your breakthrough again? Sorry for my distraction." Ms. Meryl rested her head on her hands. She wondered how perfect life would have been if she was a cloud in the sky: free of troubles, worries, and hate. But no. Her cloud-life only existed in her imagination. She was a human, a mortal, that had to deal with all the pressures of finding her very own father.

Oh, and of course she would have gone to the police if she could. She had learned that when Hilton was working as a policeman, he had actually provoked a grudge. Ms. Meryl went to the police many times, and they denied her every scrap of evidence, claiming nothing was sufficient to build a case. Someone in the police was involved in this murky porridge of a crime. She scowled at the thought a little. As if she needed all this game-playing. It was clear as the window panes in her rented house. The police were not going to help.

Dara sighed, but with her patient personality she explained again. "The four of us have come to the conclusion that Hilton is a gambler. And a **BIG** one."

Ms. Meryl shook her head in incredulity. "No! I mean, how can it be possible? Let me tell you, my father was a policeman before he retired, and he is certainly NOT the type of person that would do something like gambling."

Dara was still calm, without even a slight quiver of doubt in her voice. "I know. These kinds of findings are hard for anyone to accept. But the thing is, it's the only explanation now; we disproved all the other options."

Ms. Meryl, though unwilling, was still attempting to digest the information. "So…you claim he is a gambler?"

Dara nodded with confidence. "It appears that way, at least from our analysis currently."

"Well, that surely makes it a big breakthrough." Ms. Meryl coughed.

Dara kept talking. "The major issue now is how he managed to not spend any money in the last 2 months before he disappeared."

Ms. Meryl looked out the window. The night sky was already a darkened sapphire, and for a second she pondered how many test sheets she still had to mark before she could go back to her cozy home.

She thought she saw the glint of a grey eye staring at her, the expression unreadable but undeniably threatening. She made out the thin outline of an angular face and…a curled thin mustache? Really? She scoffed at her wild imagination. She was too stressed out. Then there was the flicker of movement of a dark shadow outside. It moved quickly, silhouetted against the bushes. The ruffle of leaves as they slid across each other was faint, but she caught it. She felt every muscle of her body tense up and tapped the table–it was her way of relieving stress. So it had not been her imagination at all.

Someone was listening to their conversation.

The figure attached to the shadow stood up abruptly and dashed out with the speed of an antelope in a stampede. Ms. Meryl and Dara were on their feet too, attempting to run out of the corridor and seize the shadow. Just about two seconds later they realized that such effort was futile. The shadow was too fast for them; they lost sight of it within seconds. The school was empty again, but not in the familiar way it was in the evenings sometimes when Ms. Meryl had to stay late. No, it was empty in a creepy way Dara had never felt before. It was…an unfamiliar and disrupting thought.

"Who was that?" Dara was nervous.

"Seriously, I don't know." Ms. Meryl wiped the sweat from her forehead.

Like broken gear wheels in a factory, the recent events felt out of place. Ms. Meryl contemplated silently as Dara left the room and headed home. Ms. Meryl had figured out a faint outline of the truth; but the outline was blurred once again into misty thought. The truth was like an object under thick ice. They were incapable of breaking it out, and couldn't quite see what it was.

In the dark, the shadow smiled with satisfaction. So they weren't able to figure it out after all. He was safe.

CHAPTER TWELVE
GRADES AND STRESS

"**N**ow I will hand out everybody's quiz results from last class," Ms. Meryl said, standing by her desk.

"Awwww," Sabrina complained as she stretched herself over her desk like an annoyed cat waiting to attack.

Rachel's face was calm when she received her test results.

"A hundred again?" Dara asked. Rachel nodded, as if it was as ordinary as going to school everyday. Well, in some ways, it was ordinary, at least for Rachel.

"Oh God, you're gonna be the first one to get a one hundred average in Biology!" Magaritte shot her a long stare of jealousy and the unbelievable feel of "Seriously? Dude, you've got to be kidding!"

Dara smiled. "I am so happy for you! Really."

Sabrina squeezed her head in between the chatting three. She silently and suddenly poked Rachel.

"Argh!" Rachel jumped a little, then fell back into her seat again.

"Sabrina! I knew it would be you!" She made a funny face by stretching out her cheeks as far as possible. She even let her tongue drop out.

"Okay guys, that's enough private review time. Let's go through the questions together now." Said Ms. Meryl. The class quieted down immediately. Ms. Meryl walked to the front of the class, and the sound of her high heels clicking echoed throughout the classroom.

"Oh…Not again…" Sabrina yawned with annoyance. Her voice stretched across the quiet classroom. Now everybody was looking at her.

"Ahem." Ms. Meryl stared coldly at Sabrina, giving her the legendary glare that the class knew as "The Shivers."

"The first section we will take a look at is phospholipid bilayers."

The class went on for what seemed like a millennia, until Sabrina's head was dropping and she tried her best not to fall asleep.

The bell rang and Sabrina jerked her head up. She had been sleeping stretched to the side, and hit her head on the windowsill. "Ow…" Sabrina scowled in pain.

~   ~   ~

Ms. Meryl hurried home, walking rapidly on the sidewalk. It had rained only a few hours earlier. In a way, Ms. Meryl had hoped it

WOULD rain, but only when she was already at home. That's exactly the reason she was gliding into the small alleyway now. Suddenly, she could feel a sharp pain in her feet due to her high heels. The weather report showed it would rain this evening, and Ms. Meryl certainly did **NOT** want to get soaked again like last time. Especially today in her new clothes. Ms. Meryl thought: "it's not fun to be seen with my hair in strands all over my face, and with my clothing dripping."

Nevertheless, she pushed the embarrassing thought out of her mind and focused on walking. Just putting one foot in front of another. Simple as that. Ms. Meryl's mind screamed as her high heels splashed into a muddy pool. Oh no. Now the muddy water was all over her ankles and feet. She hopped around in her high heels, awkwardly, like a little child trying to avoid the puddles. Ms. Meryl laughed aloud at her own absurdity.

Her feet slowed and she stopped by a small apartment. Using her keys she entered the living room. A warm, yellow light filled the whole room with pleasure. The aroma of damp sunflowers and a lasting scent of bread dough infused the room. Fortinbras, her enormous Golden Retriever and Wolfhound mix ran up to greet her with affection. She kicked off her high heels, the pair of shoes that made her feet miserable and gave her a sore back.

Ms. Meryl collapsed on the soft, puffy sofa, and gave a long sigh of relief. Finally, after a long day, she was in her cozy, little home. It was small, but it gave her extreme satisfaction and the feeling of safety.

A strand of lightning slashed across the sky ferociously, followed by the deafening drumming of thunder.

Ms. Meryl sat up. She bumped up and down softly on the fluffy pillow. She felt that she had forgotten something. The feeling that she could not retrieve the missing part of her puzzle made her annoyed.

She ignored the feeling that something big was about to happen. She rested her head on the back of the sofa, and drifted into a tranquil sleep. She couldn't recall how much time had passed since she had dozed off so serenely. Every night she tossed about in her bed, unable to enter the world of dreams. A huge cloud of enormous pressure loomed over her, making her world grey and bland, just like the worlds of other adults. But no. Today, despite the dark cloud of anxiety and annoyance, she had one moment of pure rest and joy.

In her semi-sleep she heard her alarm go off. She reluctantly opened her eyes. Being too lazy to turn her head, she stretched her arm and patted the sofa a couple of times before she was able to find her phone.

She checked her phone wearily as she stared at the message on the screen. It said:

[From Dean Allison: @Meryl, Is your device set up? We are waiting for you in the meeting.]

Oh no! The meeting! Ms. Meryl jerked upwards. She still had a meeting with all of the other staff in the school. She had totally forgotten about it! She grunted with annoyance, wrestling her laptop out of her narrow work bag. Ms. Meryl anxiously opened up her computer and typed in her password.

"What on earth is wrong with you today!" She snapped at her computer. She ruffled her golden pool of hair as she stared at the huge letters on the screen showing "Your password is incorrect."

Ms. Meryl breathed dramatically and tried to cool herself down. She typed her password letter by letter and finally got in.

She frantically processed a couple of windows and she breathed a sigh of relief. The meeting page came into view.

Mrs. Allison, the nightmare dean, opened her camera and her plump face appeared on Ms. Meryl's laptop.

"Where have you been, Ms. Meryl? Hmm? Your tardiness has caused us all to waste 12 minutes waiting for you!" Mrs. Allison bellowed at the screen as if within the next second she could jump out of Ms. Meryl's laptop and smash it into pieces.

"Oh no, I'm sorry." Ms. Meryl conceded; Mrs. Allison would continue reproaching her if she did not.

That mere apology seemed to quench Mrs. Allison's thirst quickly though. It was out of character for her. She was almost always angry at everything. But then, everyone seemed out of character these days. First there was Sabrina, who had, as if magically, developed the inspiration to study Biology, and then Dara, who seemed to soften her strong, commanding character a little and wasn't so serious about everything anymore. Rachel was still the same, a quietly gentle girl, yet something about her had also changed. Maturity, yes, that was it; she was much more mature these days and, it seemed, such growth made her even quieter–but in a different way. Before, it had been a timid tranquility, her shyness not provoking her to speak further. Now she was much more thoughtful, and often fell into long lapses of silence when she just sat there, pondering. What was going on in her mind no one knew. Magaritte–well, she seemed more sullen now, a bit unlike her previous, shining self. She had a disposition very similar to Sabrina; only that she was more logical…and reasonable, one might say with a laugh. But she seemed to shrink a little, to dry up, all that familiar liveliness evaporating from her. Family matters, I suppose, Ms. Meryl thought. And finally, there was Mrs. Allison. She was definitely changing. She wasn't as grumpy as she was previously, and now seemed more kindly. She became more amiable, and although was still profoundly annoying at times, the ice layer of long-sustained incompatibility seemed to thaw slightly.

"Alright, now listen to this. We are going to be hosting an activity, and although not all of you have mandatory participation, I expect all of you to be involved voluntarily."

How funny, Ms. Meryl thought. Being forced to "volunteer" when your work wasn't even required. She knew what this was about: hosting some Math competition at school again. Anyways, she was a Biology teacher, not a Math teacher, and hopefully no one would be picking at her for not going. Anyways, she didn't have to pay attention now. Ms. Kuby, a generous, kind-hearted woman who was one of Ms. Meryl's friends amongst the school staff, would send her all the notes afterwards.

Ms. Meryl wasn't listening. She was nodding at the screen systematically like a robot, but her thoughts had already wandered elsewhere.

She turned off her camera on her computer, hoping that she would fade in Mrs. Allison's mind and memory. Mrs. Allison's shrill yet commanding voice echoed faintly. The meeting was still going on. There were more than 150 staff members in the meeting! She didn't have to worry, Ms. Meryl told herself, no one would be bothered that her screen had gone dark.

The light of the living room dimmed, and Ms. Meryl failed to recognize that it was actually her eyes closing. She slid from drowsiness to sleep. It was the best sleep she had in 5 years, despite the bone of her arms feeling a bit hard as she rested her head upon them.

CHAPTER THIRTEEN
HILTON'S LAPTOP

"**H**ow could Hilton be a gambler?" Ms. Meryl muttered to Fortinbras. She flipped through Hilton's papers. Fortinbras cocked his head sideways and stared at Ms. Meryl with large, hypnotic dog eyes. He looked thoughtful for someone with a brain the size of a lemon.

Hilton's house was well-lit from a big window in the living room. It was also very hot. Ms. Meryl was frantically pulling off her thick sweater since she felt she would pass out the next moment in the unbearable heat. She grunted with annoyance when she hit her elbow hard on one of the book shelves to her right. Disheartened and grumpy, Ms. Meryl collapsed on the sofa. Leaning her head over in exhaustion, Ms. Meryl thought to herself, How can finding some evidence at Hilton's house be so difficult? Fortinbras mimicked Ms. Meryl and jumped on the sofa. He landed on her leg hard. She whined. I mean, after all, he was a huge dog.

~   ~   ~

Ms. Meryl felt like she was breaking down. All the pressure, annoyance, and disgust was driving her crazy.

She gazed around the room, checking everything she had searched. Well, the result was…nothing.

Suddenly, she noticed a laptop bag she had never seen before. Her heart thumped with anticipation and she slid awkwardly in her slippers when she attempted to walk faster. Ms. Meryl's hands were numb when she opened the bag. A computer. A Mac.

Ms. Meryl was about to raise her hands in victory until she realized an even bigger issue. She did not have the passcode. She could not get in. Her feeling of victory was overwhelmed by a wave of depression. She felt as if she was in deep water and frantically floundering, but not able to move as she sank deeper and deeper. It was… suffocating. The mind was screaming, pounding on invisible walls that kept her inside a box. She was like an animal in a cage. Animal in a cage. No control over her body. All she could do was wait. Wait for unconsciousness. Wait for a tingle on her skin telling her that she was okay now. Just wait.

Wait.

Wait.

Dreadful waiting.

Blue.

Darker blue.

Black.

Unconsciousness.

Pain.

Unbearable pain.

Ms. Meryl opened her eyes again.

She was once again in the living room of Hilton's house. One that originally had her father in it. Now, she was alone. Alone.

Ms. Meryl sat down. She set the computer on the table. She sighed. Maybe this would be exhausting, depressing, painful, all the feelings combined. But she had to try.

She entered his birthday. Incorrect.

Ms. Meryl tried to settle down her feelings a little.

Alright. Two more attempts to go.

She entered her birthday. Incorrect.

Ms. Meryl's heart was pounding, the vision of being drowned circled back into her mind again. But this time she opened her eyes and shook the idea out of her head.

Ms. Meryl recalled the last time they found the safety deposit box. The code inside it. His bank passcode.

She entered it. She clearly felt the push of every key in the keyboard. Her heart was thumping. Her throat seemed to be blocked by something. Her breathing started getting heavier and heavier until it was a pant.

The computer was loading.

Loading.

Loading.

Loading.

The light of the computer seemed to glow a bit brighter. The dark blue of the screen transitioned to a lighter blue hue that only darkened at the sides, as if saying: Look at me. Use me. Type.

Ms. Meryl's lips curled up in satisfaction.

She opened every app, checked every bit of history Hilton had used. Nothing important anywhere.

Ms. Meryl scrolled down the emails Hilton had received. Her eyes were focused on the screen, as if staring THROUGH the computer. Most of them were ads, but the rest of them were mostly from a man named Zach Cochlan. Ms. Meryl felt her purpose sharpen. She typed the name 'Zach' in the search bar, and lots of emails popped up.

Ms. Meryl read through them carefully, barely even daring to breathe.

Her mind spun with all the possibilities, and in a whirl of disbelief she felt dizzy. Ms. Meryl breathed heavily but slowly. She was attempting to steady herself after a day with a roller coaster of emotions.

She read through each email. She imagined every scenario.

One of them particularly stung her eyes:

"Hilt.

I am demanding my money back right now.

I will not allow you more time.

Go to The Building now. NOW. At this exact **INSTANT**. Or **FACE THE CONSEQUENCES.**

- Zach."

This was sent on February 10th, exactly one week before Hilton's disappearance.

Ms. Meryl was trembling now. She did not know whether it was fear or wrath that was controlling her. It did not matter. Five words echoed in Ms. Meryl's mind. I need to find him. **I NEED TO FIND HIM. I NEED TO FIND HIM!**

Whether she would or not, remained to be seen.

CHAPTER FOURTEEN
A DIFFERENT PERSPECTIVE

Ms. Meryl was having a really bad headache at two in the morning and she struggled on her feet, climbed out of bed, stammered a little and steadied herself. Right. Deep breath in, deep breath out. The night was at its climax now, the darkest time of the whole day. Everything was still except for the shuffling of Ms. Meryl's blankets. For some reason, she wrote a diary that night.

Here is an excerpt from Ms. Meryl's diary:

Dear Diary,

I hate my brain for having an allergy headache at 2 o'clock in the morning.

I hate Mrs. Allison for making me do her work and picking on me.

I hate teaching Biology. It's monotonous. I have taught it a billion times.

I hate having to get up everyday at 6 O'clock to mark 42 test sheets.

I hate that my father is missing, and my heart is strangling everydayfor news that he has been found.

I hate everything.

Including myself.

I wonder why that devil Dean Allison picks on me and only ME every time I go to get coffee. Maybe because Allison is in her fifties and jealous of me for being so young. Weird.

Who is **ZACH COCHLAN**? Why did he send that email to Hilton? And what on **EARTH** does "The Building" mean? **WHAT DID HILTON GO TO** "The Building" **FOR**?

@the strange questions above. Please stop disrupting my brain. You are making me very worried about Hilton now.

MY HEAD HURTS……

@Mrs. Allison. You spilled my coffee today. On my new sweater. **ACCIDENTALLY.** And you didn't offer to get it cleaned.

One more time and I'll sue you.

Yeah. I'll sue everyone in the world, I guess.

Pressure here, pressure there. Pressure pressure everywhere. Hilton is definitely a gambler, I guess, huh? That is such a contradictory phrase. "Definitely," and "I guess." Just like Mrs. Allison FORCED me to "volunteer" at Parent-Teacher Conference night. I'm a "forced" volunteer who is "definitely" guessing.

If I could choose again, I would NEVER be a teacher. There is just lots and lots of work after work. I don't just work, I also do homework. Think about it! Teachers are NEVER the ones who get the most praise in society, yet they have so much work to do! Even on holidays. And Mrs. Allison is a sneaky mean walrus!

Ugg. Thinking of the police again.

Huh. Isn't it ridiculous? They are now just as reluctant as ever! Yet when the police sergeant's daughter's favorite dog was lost they actually sent the whole team and searched the town for any signs of her. Now my father's gone and they're like "Oh it's okay he's having a grudge, hey? He'll come back someday."

Right. Mustached little guy. I'll tear your head off then if he doesn't.

Basically a month ago my dad just "vaporized," according to the police. The police filed a report but nothing happened. Clearly something is wrong. I don't trust the police. There are rumors about internal affairs investigating corruption. I can't trust anything at all.

Suddenly I'm so worried. Well, I wasn't so worried before because I thought it was just a temper tantrum and he didn't want to talk to me. It's all because we got into an argument two weeks before his disappearance and I wasn't worried, but now it's really getting serious.

@myself-. Go to sleep immediately, or I suppose I'll have a stroke tomorrow.

Reply@myself: Nah. My head hurts too much.

@: I don't wanna have a stroke.

Reply@: Of course you do. At least you can get a couple days off. You won't have to see The Walrus Dean Allison. Yay.

@: She's not that bad.

Reply@: WHAT! That's an absolute NO! She didn't even offer to pay to clean my new sweater and she smirked when she spilled my coffee.

@: Dunno. Don't care. Now GO TO SLEEP!

Reply@: Stop sounding like my mom. We're part of the same being, so I get to make a fair share of the decisions too. We're both Lily Elizabeth Meryl, so I can decide that we are NOT going to sleep.

@: Fine fine. At least my part of the brain has already slept.

Reply@: Doesn't matter. I'm gonna get some coffee and stay up, it's an opportunity to get an early start!

@: [Yawn] An early start? On what? What opportunity? An opportunity to get a heart attack? And you're drinking caffeine? At this time? Anyways. Stop keeping me up. I'm gonna sleep now, so shut up!   @: zzzzzzzzzzzzzzzzzzzzzzz

OMG. I'm talking to myself. I guess now I really am crazy.

Where's the nearest hospital?

Lol.

Lily Elizabeth Meryl, I am serious now, and demand you to go to sleep!

My. Head. Hurts. OMG. Someone. **SAVE. ME FORTINBRAS!!!! STOP BARKING!** My head's gonna **EXPLODE.**

I **HATE** allergy attacks.

Ow. It's so painful and **SOOOO ITCHY!**

Reply to myself: I guess I'll lose sleep again tonight. No one sleeps well under these conditions.

OH NO. I got a rash now.

I look as red as a tomato.

Sort of funny, but actually not funny at all.

Who on earth is scratching at my window! Stop it, or I will sue you.

Please stop scratching. Wait…Did Hilton tell me before that scratching means…but who would…

[Ms. Meryl's dairy ends here]

CHAPTER FIFTEEN
THE MAN

Only a few hours later, but quite a distance away, a very different scene unfolded...

"Give me her address!"

The Man's voice echoed through the suddenly eerie basement. For a moment he was shocked by the hostility of his own voice. It did not sound like him, it was as if another soul had taken over him. But he had no choice. Hilton caused all of this. Even if the sky fell down on top of him now it would be Hilton's fault. Hilton was at fault for everything, he thought, as he trembled slightly.

"I will not!" Hilton's voice was muffled though understandable under the tape covering his mouth.

"How dare you!" Wrath was controlling The Man, sinking deeper and deeper into his soul until it made a scar there. He pointed a dagger at Hilton. He was shaking as his face was distorted into an unreadable expression. For a moment Hilton saw desperation and helplessness in his eyes. But it vanished. It returned to malice and hate.

The Man never intended to kill Hilton, he knew. It would be too quick, too easy a death for him. He wanted Hilton to suffer, to suffer horribly. To suffer even more than The Man's own mother. He wanted the desperation to eat its way right through Hilton's soul, leaving a cavity there as big as the one in The Man's heart.

"I WILL NOT!" Hilton was shaking, and even he did not know whether it was fear, anger, hate, or just simply a reflex. He knew clearly the consequences of speaking against The Man. But no. It wasn't just Hilton's own safety he was worried about: he had her to think about. He would not risk her safety with a foolish action. He needed to protect her. He would do everything and anything to complete that job.

The figure dropped his dagger. Hilton could only see his outline under the dim light, and the shadow was breathing hard as his chest rose and fell.

Hilton's heart thumped. He could feel the pulse in his throat, and he tried to swallow the beat away. It was agonizing. Something seemed to block his throat. His hands were tied, and he could not free them. The loss of oxygen was severe now. His face went pale. A reflex told him to frantically jerk the ropes off. He tried, but they were stiff.

The figure seemed to be contemplating something. He smirked at Hilton while watching him trying to break free. He laughed quietly but coldly.

"Foolish drama," he murmured, "one day I will figure it out myself."

He turned off the lights and slammed the door of the basement as he left.

In the dark, Hilton was still struggling.

~   ~   ~

The Man stared at the address book intently under a yellowish light.

He intensified his look on that name: Hilton Meryl.

He traced his finger tentatively over that name again and again and a malicious smile curled up on his face. The smile didn't belong to him. It wasn't him. But he didn't care now. It did not appear to him that he had changed: life had eroded him and reshaped him again. His fingers were rough; his skin was tanner than the last time he had seen himself in the mirror…But those changes were minor, ones that followed with age. Moreover, his personality had changed—his soul. It wasn't colorful like it had been in childhood, and perhaps it would never be again. He was strange, a hostile being. If he was capable of realizing it, he would have been shocked by his own actions.

Fury replaced his once-kind personality again as he recalled the smell of the hospital: a suffocating mix of medicine and sanitizer. He had dashed into the room. He had held her old hand and squeezed it repeatedly. He was helpless as he prayed and whispered into his mother's hand. A nurse forced him out of the room. He was desperate. Seeing his mother lying in bed, unable to move, outside the window. He banged his hand on the window. He could not pay his bills when he needed to. He sent a message to his cousins. He sent a message to Hilton for his money back. No one replied. He was clenching his own hands in his helplessness. But it was too late now. It was his own fault. In some way it wasn't, but then, still, they were his own actions.

Then it was all over.

Her breathing had stopped. Her face was serene.

The last time he saw her. The last time he ever would.

Now, in the dim room, he seemed to see his mother again. Her wrinkled but gentle face. Her weathered, old hands. He reached out to grab them, to hold her—but there was nothing.

Alone. Again.

Tears rolled down and drenched the page of the address book. He was so scared. So desperate. So helpless. He knew he would get arrested soon. He could even see the freezing, metal bars of a jail cell. He had a suffocating sense he would be caught. The sun passed down behind the hills, and all that was left to provide him company was darkness. And what had humanity done?

Allow Hilton to be a lying gambler.

He came back to reality. His hands had been clutching the pages of the book, and when he relaxed his hold, a page of paper was crumpled and tattered. Exactly like his very own experience: monotonous but tattered, varied but melancholy, previously colorful thoughts had become simply different shades of gray. Nothing more. Sometimes he considered himself a failure. He was unique, but only based on the fact that he was so far apart from the rest of society. Every human being seemed nice, but combined together…humanity was a devouring shadow, a monster, the being of evil itself. Just like a group of people staring at one individual. Everyone had only contributed one pair of eyes, but combined would be a thousand pairs. Everyone is innocent, yet in a way they were all guilty of something, something very vague. Yet still, they were all guilty. One drop of water won't do any harm, but a million droplets hanging on to each other—a wave of devastation, of criticism, of disgust, of abominable statements. Men had created each other for the sake of the destruction of one another.

He sat deep in thought. He had rested his chin on a hand, and was looking up at the ceiling.

He forcefully pushed the philosophy out and set his ideas on another matter. His mother. And The Man responsible for his mother's death. Hilton Meryl. And now he would suffer.

Once again, the scenes of the pain on his mother's face when she had died flowed back to his mind. The healing scar in his heart split open again, and this time it left even a bigger slash. In a sudden surge of pain, he lunged forward and held the left side of his chest. He breathed heavily, but with each motion his heart pounded even more. It felt like a million pins in his chest. He held his breath, but it did not last for long. With each move he made, his heart ached.

He collapsed on his bed. The sudden attack had left every inch of him aching. His throat was dry. He tried to moan, but no sound came out. Only the feel of blood in his throat. He coughed, and the pressure made his ears hurt.

He just lay there, focusing himself only on his breathing.

His eyelids weighed heavier, and slowly he began closing them.

He fell asleep.

In his dreams he was once again in the dandelion field with his mother. The field that was once part of his father's farm. He could still recall clearly how young his mother was at the time! His mother was wearing the dress with yellow flowers on it, the one that she liked best. She blew a dandelion at him, and he giggled. There were only the two of them, and an endless view of dandelions. The breeze tickled at his plump little face. He felt as if he was in one of Monet's paintings. The breeze blew his mother's grand golden hair and her dress puffed out. It was…beautiful.

She turned around then. But her face suddenly blurred, and he could not see it clearly, no matter how much he blinked. He reached out to clasp her hand, but she was no longer there. His memories suddenly seemed so vague, so far away, as if they had never ever happened.

He blinked.

He was awake again, once again returned to his damp, old room.

Memories of his mother only brought him fury. How she had died…

This was all HILTON's fault. His body shook in anger now. The room became a wave of fire, and he was in the exact center of it. He moved out of bed, and raised up the address book. He smashed it on the ground. The spine of the book folded, making it look suddenly so old. He saw the glass cup. A whirl of motion.Spinning. Black. Dizziness. He didn't realize what was happening. He felt his head throb, and it suddenly felt so heavy. He felt like he was going to topple over the next moment.

He had thrown the cup on the ground.

The cup splintered into hundreds of bits of broken glass. The shattering sound it made seemed like pins, stabbing through his ears.

He screamed. For no exact reason. But also for every reason in life.

He kneeled on the ground.

He collected the small bits of glass and held them up towards the light. The sharp bits slashed his hands, but he did not care. He couldn't even feel the pain. Nothing seemed to matter to him now.

Blood dripped from his palm, and he stared calmly at his bloody hands.

He stared up at the ceiling and promised himself, the way he had done every time he thought of his mother.

This was all Hilton's fault. He said to himself for perhaps the one thousandth time, And he's going to pay for it.

CHAPTER SIXTEEN
ACTION

The Man waited in the bushes.

Ms. Meryl went inside her house, and the door closed with a long yawn.

The Man sprang into action.

Fortinbras barked at him.

He made a gesture that said "silence!" Then he held the meatball in his hands and slowly crumbled it on the ground.

Fortinbras stared at him. The dog bent down and sniffed the bits of meat.

Eat it, The Man thought, eat it!

Fortinbras looked up again. He did not eat the meat. He growled. He growled deeper, and now he was focused on The Man in front of him. The fur on his back stood up, and his ears pricked. Fortinbras bared his teeth and stepped forward towards The Man. Fortinbras' fur seemed so bright, and it almost glowed in the moonlight. But it only lasted for an instant. Perhaps it was just a trick of the shadows.

Fortinbras stood up fully, and his massive shadow stretched beyond the dry grass surrounding him. He snarled.

Threatened, the figure backed off into the darkness.

Fortinbras stared at the meat after he left. He pushed it away with his front paw, rejecting eating it like any other dog would have.

Apparently, Fortinbras was not just any dog. He had a much more sensitive nose and mind than most. And the meat, he could tell, was poisoned…

CHAPTER SEVENTEEN
FORTINBRAS

It was a breezy day, and the sun was hidden behind the faint gray clouds. A light wind ruffled Ms. Meryl's blond hair, which was short at the time.

Ms. Meryl was only 20 years old. She was an undergraduate at Amherst College and heading home after a tiring day of Biology lab reports.

Evening settled in more quickly than she had expected it. The street lights lit up together in gorgeous harmony. Ms. Meryl quickened her pace.

She gripped her unfinished report tightly. She was bringing it home to complete, feeding her anxious need to turn it in early.

When she raised up her head a moment before to check the state of the sky, it was a relaxing shade of light blue. Now, she turned again to find a magnificent sight. The sky was beginning to darken at the horizon into an elegant blue, one you would find if you stared into the core of a sapphire. At that exact moment she was outlined by a thin thread of golden sunlight. If only someone would admire the harmonious beauty of the scene! The sun slipped below the hill, and in its place was a street illuminated by blurred street lamps. Now it was a classic sight: a young woman striding down the street under lonely streetlights. Hers was a solitary, distinct beauty.

Ms. Meryl turned at the corner. In the middle of the road was a large dog. He was dirty with matted fur.

The dog stared at Ms. Meryl with both pleading and curious eyes, and she stared back. If you were to look intently, (which would be difficult under the dim light of the streetlights,) you would see that the big dog had a rich golden coat stained with mud and small bits of grass.

The dog followed Ms. Meryl. It was not in a rush, but it gave a small trot, as if both taking its time and awaiting an answer. The soft pads of its feet made small, satisfying noises on the weathered concrete of the road.

Ms. Meryl was puzzled, but deep in her heart, she felt a growing sense of familiarity. She wanted to bring the dog home, though she did not know if she should be afraid of it. But something in her instinct, in her gut, told her that the dog was seeking help. Her soul was attracted, and the feeling of sympathy swelled.

She knelt down slightly, just at the same height of the dog. As if awaiting a definite response, the dog moved forward two small steps and raised its head high. Ms. Meryl held out a hand. As if from innate behavior, the dog walked forward. It seemed to understand her gesture, to be able to see through her and read her mind.

This was no ordinary dog, Ms. Meryl thought. Its intelligence had been revealed a moment ago, when it had understood what Ms. Meryl really meant by holding out a hand: that she accepted it, and that it was welcome to join her as a member of her family.

A faint smile danced on Ms. Meryl's face, and she could not explain exactly why. The smile was so sincere, even for a college student pushed to her limits of weariness and integrity. It was not a fake smile required for a picture, but the type of smile expressed by the heart. Her SOUL was smiling.

As if corresponding to her suddenly improved mood, the seemingly exhausted lights suddenly burst into liveliness, they lit up so brightly that Ms. Meryl had to shut her eyes tight when the outburst happened.

The big dog trotted next to her, not jumping up and down like other dogs, not whimpering or barking. He moved silently, his intriguing and deep eyes focused on the road in front of him. Ms. Meryl had sensed his uniqueness, his intelligence, and also his integrity. Ms. Meryl had a hint of a feeling that it was something from his past that had shaped him this way.

The two of them, a girl and a dog, walked silently along the sidewalk. Fortinbras had a more vivid past than even Ms. Meryl sensed, more vivid than anyone would imagine.

~   ~   ~

It was three years ago. Ms. Meryl typed away in her cozy room. It was dimly lit by a small lamp. One hand on her computer, Ms. Meryl stretched out the other to pet Fortinbras, who was at her side. The room was toasty, and though the heating was old, it still did a fine job warming up the room. Fortinbras was tired. He slowly closed his eyes as he reimagined the brightness of the sun on the balcony today that gave his fur a tip of light.

Fortinbras dreamed, and he was too sound asleep to hear Ms. Meryl chuckling at him when he raised his ears or pawed at the ground in his sleep. It was normal to him, of course; he had dreamed about finding a big bone!

Even now, Fortinbras often dreams about Bryan and Lila and the beautiful small farm they once lived on together. Bryan and Lila were his previous two owners before he got lost one night, and they owned a farm in a rural area of Massachusetts. Lila was Bryan's daughter.

In his dream, Fortinbras was in the green fields in front of the farm; Bryan was on the porch of the farm chatting away with Lila. Fortinbras saw a golden butterfly, and he followed it…

Fortinbras felt the sun on his fur. A gentle breeze ruffled through the fine fur on his back, and he sat down on the ground, feeling the wind. He saw Bryan; an old man in his mid 80s, optimistic, the type that always laughed it off. But Fortinbras knew him deeply; he could read the worry behind his shrug when, many years ago, the flood damaged his crops; or when the storm blew his collection of seeds away. Oh yes, Fortinbras knew all too well about the old man's worries. But Bryan always had a smile there for someone that needed it more desperately than him. And Fortinbras had been a good companion.

They often played Frisbee together, in the fields, at dusk, with the last pieces of sunlight. They enjoyed the golden moments of dusk together often, and Bryan always accompanied this peace with a hearty laugh. When only the very last fraction of the sun could be seen across the hill, Bryan would yank the Frisbee from Fortinbras, laughing, and call for home. Bryan would drag a tired Fortinbras home for supper, back into the small-though-cozy cottage they shared. Bryan always filled Fortinbras' bowl to the brim with dog food, and the living room always had its usual hint of the aroma of cinnamon. Bryan, a skilled carpenter with daily interactions with wood, had the talent to make Fortinbras his own little bed. Fortinbras would occasionally snuggle on his cushion until the sun was high up in the sky, and Bryan would give him a few sips of milk as a special treat when he finally woke up. It refreshed Fortinbras, the still warm goat milk, but he couldn't have too much. Bryan woke up way earlier than Fortinbras most of the time, but sometimes Fortinbras woke up at the same time as him and trotted into the fields with him, too.

In his dream, Fortinbras recalled the house full of the attractive aroma of turkey on Thanksgiving one year, and how he stood in the kitchen bouncing up and down, trying his best not to drool. That year he had tried to steal the whole Turkey, but ended up with only one leg. Bryan chuckled, but still gave him a very non-serious scolding. Bryan's whole family was crowded there, and many people had laughed at the affectionate and hilarious behavior between man and dog. Lila was there too, and Fortinbras remembered her laugh from that special Thanksgiving— a laugh where her eyes lit up along with her voice.

He remembered the day when Bryan died, he was not able to understand what happened to him. He jumped anxiously by his bed. The day was gray and stormy, and the oak trees outside were all distorted, blown out of shape. It was raining outside, and the droplets of water pounded against the glass windows and the roof. Thunder and lighting, as if by mere coincidence, happened at the exact same time, and a deafening roar of nature's beast added on to the blinding slash of light that cut the sky in half.

Fortinbras was startled. He jumped in his dream, and hit the nearby table hard. In his dream, Fortinbras saw Lila come through the door in a hurry. Even with a raincoat on, she was soaked, and her brown hair was stuck to her back. Fortinbras remembered that Lila had weariness in her eyes. Lila took a look at Bryan, and quickly fumbled to grab her phone. She held her breath, not allowing fear to pass through her. She called the ambulance. Fortinbras knew it was too late. But Bryan had died peacefully.

Fortinbras licked Bryan's hands again. He was hoping Bryan would wake up, laugh, and say it was a trick. No. Bryan didn't. After what seemed like a long time for Fortinbras, the ambulance arrived. Fortinbras remembered lots of people were crowded into the small room, and he was scared. In his memory, he had ducked under Bryan's desk, and cuddled himself into a ball. A group of people dressed in white took Bryan away, and Lila was too busy to notice Fortinbras wandering out of the room. Fortinbras sniffed the night air, and he suddenly felt everything was so different. Fortinbras saw the desperation in Lila's eyes. He remembered that when the crowd of people had left, Lila had crouched on the ground and sobbed. He had stayed near her. In his dream and memory, the storm pounded on, and Bryan's room suddenly was no longer cozy to Fortinbras. The place he dwelled in the most now seemed as cold and unfamiliar as a stranger.

Bryan's funeral was on a freezing winter day. Fortinbras still remembers the slicing, sharp wind blowing at his face. The wind was blasting cold and felt like a knife on his ears. Fortinbras tried to snuggle and warm himself up, but nothing worked. He was not able to understand death, but he sensed the grief in the air. He knew something was wrong, and that Bryan was in trouble. He did not see Bryan and had a shadowy feeling that he never would again. Fortinbras recalled his helplessness. He needed Bryan. Bryan, who was always there for anybody that needed help, who was always there to solve any issues, however serious, was now gone.

Then Fortinbras' dream moved on to Lila. Ah, yes, his life with Lila. Fortinbras had been passed to Lila after Bryan died. Lila had a family, and she had a decent husband and two children who liked Fortinbras a lot. Fortinbras enjoyed his time with Lila, yet never felt he was part of the family. He was treated like a friend, a visitor, not as a family member. He was lacking the feeling of belonging that he had always had with Bryan's broad smile and big hug.

Lila was a detective. She was busy, though she would sometimes (if she had time) train and play with Fortinbras on the weekends. Her training revealed Fortinbras' innate ability to retrieve objects. Yes, Fortinbras' bowl was still always filled to the brim with dog food. But he never enjoyed the golden light of dusk again with Bryan, nor did he jump and trot in such a carefree manner like he did when he was with Bryan.

Fortinbras remembered Lila's smile. In his memory, he could still clearly see the shine in her eyes when she smiled that Thanksgiving. At home, though, after she took over raising Fortinbras, she did not smile that much. Her life was painted gray, and real smiles from the soul, common in childhood, were suddenly so rare.

Fortinbras felt a warm, soft, glaze of sunshine. He lifted his head, without opening his eyes. He listened to the chirp of small birds outside. He then slowly opened his eyes.

It was all a dream, yet it was all derived from the most familiar memories…

CHAPTER EIGHTEEN
FEAR

Ms. Meryl returned home. She was tired. For an unknown reason the streetlights weren't working today, yet they had been working fine since Ms. Meryl moved into the house. The lights flickered quickly, and it was odd, for someone had been working on them just a few days ago.

Ms. Meryl shuddered. The street was empty, but it would normally be full of people each minding their own business. Strangely, the street was totally empty today. The shops were closed. The pavement had no one on it.

Ms. Meryl felt odd. The moonlight shone eerily on the street, and goosebumps rose on her skin. She tried pushing the frightening thoughts out of her mind, but the more she tried, the bigger they got.

Ms. Meryl breathed heavily. She could take it no more. Gripping her bag in one hand, she dashed home.

She felt shadows behind her.

"It's just a trick of the shadows." She muttered to herself, aloud.

Soon she arrived at her rented house. She fumbled with the key, anxiously. She had to hold it with two hands to keep herself from trembling. She clumsily stuck it in the keyhole and turned it. The door opened with a click. She turned her head and looked around. After quickly making sure no one was there, she hurried inside. The door slammed shut.

Ms. Meryl breathed a sigh of relief as she entered the living room. Fortinbras ran up to greet her. She collapsed on the sofa, and closed her eyes wearily.

~ ~ ~

Ms. Meryl woke up. The room was dark. The lights had been turned off.

Ms. Meryl squinted and tried her best to remember. She whispered, "I don't think I turned the lights off." Darkness surrounded her.

Fear was overtaking Ms. Meryl. She quickly rose to her feet and reached for the walls, feeling for the light switch.

The wind screamed outside, shrill.

Ms. Meryl froze right on the spot.

Scratching sounds.

Ms. Meryl recalled the last time the same scratching sounds happened at her window. That time she had been distracted by a severe allergy headache.

The scratching continued.

~   ~   ~

He hid in the bushes. This time though, his goal was different. He had heard of this object before. He had even searched. He knew, this time for sure, what he wanted. It was the amulet.

The Man smiled. It was a malicious smile. The moonlight skimmed over him but passed quickly.

He walked around the house, as if taking his time.

He slowly wandered to the window of the living room. He had studied the house. He knew every inch of it by heart.

He found the window. Slowly The Man dragged out a pin from his bag and used it to scratch on the window. He wanted to scare Ms. Meryl, to threaten her, and a peculiar sort of satisfaction overcame him. He would not acknowledge the fact that she was innocent. Never. She was the daughter of Hilton Meryl–he let bitter thoughts rest upon the mere mention of his name–so she was related to guilt, too. He scratched. The crisp sound got louder and louder.

~   ~   ~

Ms. Meryl stumbled and reached for the light switch. It switched on. Ms. Meryl sighed with relief and took a glimpse at the clock. 1:47am. It was pitch-black outside. The only thing visible from the window was the reflection of the light from the room. Outside was darkness.

Ms. Meryl suddenly sat up. Something was very wrong. The empty streets…the scratching…Small droplets of sweat were forming on her brow. Ms. Meryl was frantic. She made an attempt to scream, but her throat was dry, so parched she felt strangled. She could not make a sound.

Ms. Meryl's heart thumped. She felt nowhere was safe in this house. She had nowhere to go. She dashed upstairs to her bedroom without her slippers.

Her room felt damp. Ms. Meryl reached for the light. She climbed into bed and covered herself with the blanket.

The wind howled outside. It came to a sudden stop. All there was in the room to accompany her was darkness and silence.

~   ~   ~

He saw her go upstairs into her room. He breathed in heavily. Now it was time to begin.

Outside, he walked to the other side of the house.

Slowly he took out a rope from his bag. He threw the rope onto a ledge by the window on the second floor. He shook the rope adeptly and it tied into a knot on one end hanging on the corner. Ensuring his grip with one hand, he hung on to the rope and climbed up.

He reached the second floor. He dragged the rope up and slid it back into his bag. Then he took out a small wrench.

He studied the window for a while. He knew where it led—Ms. Meryl's work room. The window was easy to break into. He took out a glass-cutter and used it to draw a small square on the window. Then he traced the square again. The small piece of glass fell forward, and he caught it with his hand. He picked at the bottom of the window with his wrench, where there was a tiny metal plate. The plate led to the hinge, which was built facing the side of the inner room to ensure protection. But the hinge was loose from age and part of it's base, a tiny copper plate, stuck out a little. With deftness and precision he pushed

He reached into his bag again and brought out a wire. He tied the wire into knots and reached his hand into the square that had been cut out. He used the wire and picked the lock.

The window opened. Carefully he raised it up and climbed in. He had not made a sound. Or so he thought.

He looked around. Ms. Meryl's workplace was tidy. He looked for the safety deposit box.

Ms. Meryl woke up. She did not know the time. Slowly she lifted the blanket and peeked out with one eye.

Click.

She heard it.

She froze. Goosebumps rose on her skin.

She felt the presence of another being in her house.

She was frantic. Under the blanket she held her breath.

She could almost hear her heart beating.

Ms. Meryl felt a small trickle of cold air reaching inside the house.

Instinctually, she knew that someone had opened the window.

She was trembling.

She did not know what she should do, or even, what she COULD do. Scream? Go and find the person who was breaking in? Hide under the blanket? Sleep?

Thousands of questions and thoughts whirled in her head all at once, and she felt dizzy.

She closed her eyes and listened. In the yard, through the shuffling sound of wind through the leaves, she heard footsteps. They were so quiet they almost felt silent. They would have been silent to anybody else, but not Ms. Meryl. She had extraordinary instincts and superb hearing.

The quiet footsteps stopped. Then they started again. And they felt nearer and nearer…

~   ~   ~

He moved away the objects on top of the box. He smiled grimly as he ran his hands over it. He lifted the box.

The box had a 4-number lock on it.

The Man pressed his ear against the surface of the box. He started turning the first column of numbers and stopped when he heard a barely audible click. He repeated the process and matched the four numbers up.

He pressed the button in the middle. The box opened.

~   ~   ~

Ms. Meryl knew where the person was. She was sure of it. In her study.

The moon was now hidden behind blackish-gray clouds. Its pale light was now feeble. The whole town seemed to dim. Ms. Meryl sat up a little, quietly, careful not to make a sound. She peered out. The streets were still empty. In the distance all the houses were dark. Not one house had turned on a light.

The whole world was dark.

A faraway crow cawed.

The only light source was a street light, the only one still lit.

Ms. Meryl climbed back to bed.

~   ~   ~

The Man slowly opened the safety deposit box. He knew what

would be in it even without looking. Before the box even totally opened, pure joy spread across The Man's face.

The Man stared into the box, numb. He studied it a bit more, flipping it up and down, looking for the amulet. But there was nothing in the box, only the velvet used to hold the amulet. The amulet was gone. Missing.

The Man's shoulders sank like a suddenly falling mountain. He could not hide his disappointment—his eyes said everything. Slowly he put everything back in place, then went out the window.

He walked down the street. It was past midnight now, almost three o'clock. A distant clock chimed, deep but solemn. The edges of the sky were starting to have a reddish glow, though it was not obvious behind the clouds. The Man was numb. The missing amulet had caught him off guard. He did not even expect it. The amulet was priceless, but it seems that it was well-protected. For a moment he even thought that HE was the one in the trap, that HE was the actual target. But he quickly thought through it and brushed the ridiculous idea from his mind. He was the one who started this. He was in control. Not anybody else. Still, all that work for nothing, was quite upsetting.

The Man walked back along the path he came in by, hands in his pockets, cautiously avoiding every source of light. It was his career, and he was an expert at it.

He arrived at his truck, which he parked far away from the populated areas of the town, and drove out. He blew on his hands. Even the gloves weren't able to keep them warm. He started the car, and the engine started its deep hum again. He drove onto a small road, not the main streets, and headed back.

He frowned in the car, one hand on the steering wheel and the other lazily holding a cigarette. The plan did not work out today. He must find another way. Maybe, only maybe, he could get his target to come to him.... He wanted to have his lamb come to the slaughter…

Incoming call
Unknown

CHAPTER NINETEEN
BROKEN PIECES

It was a cloudy day. Not very cold, though there was no sun. The sky was a gloomy gray, as if it was in a bad mood.

Ms. Meryl went to monitor a student-volunteer movie studying activity at the cinema. She had been forced to, although forced in the name of volunteering. It wasn't even vaguely "voluntary." It was a BBC movie about aquatic life on Earth, and since she had watched it so many times it wasn't even faintly interesting to her.

The movie ended, it was bland and tedious. The students finished all their reports and handed them to her. Ms. Meryl fumbled with them a little, then stuck them inside a broken folder with edges that were torn and stuck out. She forced everything into her bag. When it wouldn't fit, she crumpled the stubborn folder with such anger and it fit in just as she was about to explode. Just when she was about to leave, she felt something sharp beneath her heels. Slowly she turned her head down and checked it out.

It was something green. A translucent green. It looked something like a broken piece of glass. Ms. Meryl's heart tightened. She knelt down and held it up. She raised it up and let the feeble light of the cinema pass through it. Not one ray was scattered.

Ms. Meryl's heart thumped. She studied it more. The broken piece had an 'Mer' on it. Ms. Meryl mumbled to herself, "Wait…This looks so familiar…" The other people watching the movie had all left, collected in small clusters like ants. Ms. Meryl was the only one left in the cinema.

A piece of memory suddenly ran across Ms. Meryl's thoughts. She recalled the night she spent with Sabrina and the other three girls. She had taken them to Hilton's house. She had opened the safety deposit box that should be holding Hilton's heirloom, the amulet. Afterwards she took it to her house. But Ms. Meryl felt something was missing from that piece of memory, and it was not complete. It was a long time ago, she just couldn't recall it…She felt like she was underwater, she needed to know but she couldn't remember. She frowned, annoyed.

It was getting late. Ms. Meryl scooped the small green piece up. She poked her head around, trying to search for other clues. She found other small broken pieces around her chair. She collected all of them and put them in the little box she used to keep her earrings. She stuck the box in her bag and headed home.

It started raining. The sky seemed especially dark because of the gloomy weather. Ms. Meryl sighed. She was tired, though she was not sure why. Wearily, she opened her umbrella. A gale of wind blasted her way. Suddenly her good mood was washed away and instantly replaced by a bad one. She shuddered and started the walk home, rain was pelting her umbrella.

~　　　　~　　　　~

Ms. Meryl arrived home. Outside the front door, she closed the umbrella. She shook it a couple of times to get the water out. Droplets flew everywhere. She stomped on the carpet in front of the door to make sure her shoes were dry, and went into the house.

Ms. Meryl was cold, but glad to be home. The warmth of the house and the strong, spicy scent of tulips from her candles soothed her. She took a deep breath and enjoyed the sting of the flowers that soothed her tired mind. She put on her slippers and headed upstairs for a hot bath.

Ms. Meryl felt much better after the bath. She was wearing her soft pajamas and collapsed on the sofa. She lay there, stretching for a while. Suddenly she jerked up. She still had work to do.

She took out the broken pieces that she collected at the cinema of what seemed like jade. She tried to piece them together. They did not fit.

She frowned. The color of the pieces weren't the light, translucent color of jade. Jade was a more minty, milky color. These pieces were…greener, brighter shade of green, and clearer. It was more transparent than the jade and showed certain marks when put under light. Wait…the marks were carvings! A wave of odd nostalgia hit Ms. Meryl, like a cold wave splashing her sleepiness into pieces.

The fragments all seemed so familiar, as if piecing a puzzle together from a dream… It was Hilton's amulet!

Suddenly she remembered. That day, the day she took Sabrina and the others to Hilton's house, the amulet was gone. Hilton had violated the family rule by wearing it out. But why… The events started to connect in an eerie way. Why would the amulet be broken? Or even, in the cinema? Did this have anything to do with the break-in at her house last week? She had heard threatening scratching sounds. And surely the amulet had great value. It was an heirloom from her great-grandfather. The jade itself was very valuable, not to mention the detailed carvings on it. Perhaps the intruder somehow knew about the amulet, and was searching for it…

But how did they know about the amulet? Ms. Meryl did not know, and that feeling crushed her. Her stomach churned with a bad feeling of anticipation…

Ms. Meryl's phone rang, interrupting her thoughts.

"Hello?" She picked up the phone.

No one spoke on the other end. There was only silence.

Ms. Meryl asked again, "Hello?"

The other person still didn't answer. Ms. Meryl lost her patience, and announced loudly: "Look, if this is some kind of annoying telemarketing, I'm suing you for selling my personal information." No response came from the other side. Ms. Meryl, her anger suddenly increasing, hit the 'End Call' button hard, and threw her phone on the sofa. She sighed. There she lay, on the sofa, gazing at the ceiling, trying to make sense of everything.

She just lay there for who-knows-how-long. She was sort of adrift; half asleep. One part of her was still in the real world, but the other was already in dreamland. After a period of time to awaken herself, Ms. Meryl sat up.

It was already dark outside. And cold. And it was raining. Which made Ms. Meryl's house now seem cozier than ever.

Ms. Meryl thought about it, frowning. She heard the sound of rain droplets hitting the window. She stood up and walked to the kitchen counter. She took a piece of paper and started drawing a diagram.

The amulet was supposed to be kept in the box. But Hilton took it out. And that violated the family rule. Hilton was kidnapped. There was a break-in last week. An intruder was looking for something. There were amulet pieces found on the cinema floor.

The intruder was looking for the amulet! And Hilton had lost it at the cinema when he wore it out! But why? Why would he wear it out? On top of that, how would Hilton lose it from around his neck?

There could only be one answer: he was kidnapped there.

Her phone rang again. Ms. Meryl stared for a second at the number, then sighed as she reached out her hand to grab it. She recognized the number. It was the same one that had bothered her before.

"Hello?" Ms. Meryl asked, not even trying to hide the weariness in her voice.

Still, no sound came from the other end. Ms. Meryl was just about to hang up again when she heard a faint whine. It seemed to be in the background of the other end. Tightly pressing her ear against the phone, Ms. Meryl quickly turned the volume up to the maximum.

"Li— Lily Elizabeth…" Ms. Meryl heard some faint words in the background. They were more like whispers than speaking. Ms. Meryl reflected for some time before her eyes rounded with shock, hardly believing it. Only her dad used her middle name. It was

Hilton's voice!

Ms. Meryl gasped out loud. She scrambled up. All the drowsiness washed away in that moment. He was alive! She was about to speak when she froze. The person on the other end of the phone had hung up. Ms. Meryl just sat there, numbly, going over what just happened.

A crystal-clear tear dropped onto her pajamas. It was cold.

Without thinking it over in her head, Ms. Meryl dialed the number back. She waited. Anticipated. Then, the repeating sound of the robot again. "Sorry, the subscriber you have dialed is busy now…Sorry, the subscriber you have dialed is busy now."

She kept her mouth covered in astonishment. She dialed 9-1-1 on her phone, but just couldn't bring herself to hit the 'call' button. She felt that something wasn't right. In fact, her instincts told her it was totally wrong. She remembered, now, how the police had been extremely reluctant to help her from the start. Especially the skinny man with a mustache. He had scolded her very subtly. And she knew his name, it was something…She couldn't quite remember. It was Zach something… Zach Cochlan? That did ring a bell in her head.

Hilton had told her, ages ago, that he had a friend named Zach. They were very good friends, at least in Ms. Meryl's memory. She remembered faintly that when she was younger, Hilton called some of his friends to watch a baseball game at his house, on TV.

She happened to be there to collect some of the old books Hilton didn't want anymore, to donate to her school. She met Zach in passing. Even through a fuzzy memory, she remembered he had tanned skin and rare, greenish-blue eyes. Who knows? The name could just be a coincidence. There are lots of people named Zach, all over the world. But…her instinct was fighting through her doubt. The skinny police officer with a mustache was tanned too…

A tear ran down her cheek silently, and landed on her pajamas.

Fury burned inside. She felt so small, so helpless. The police had an attitude so strong she could do nothing to change it. Their reluctance. Their smirks. But what could she do? Feel vengeful? That was all. The good reputation of the police seemed to shield them from the reality of their actual carelessness...

She hated the police. Why waste time with them? Even her house had been broken into, and the police weren't going to do anything about the investigation. Part of her knew that the person who broke into her house was the kidnapper, or someone working with the kidnapper. The target of that break-in, Ms. Meryl suspected, was the jade amulet, for the only way anyone could know about it is from Hilton. And, in fact, Hilton did wear it out when he shouldn't have that day, to show off to his friends. Maybe the abductor wanted to break in and steal the amulet after they found out about it. And the police were weird too. It angered her to think of such unjust corruption while her father was still missing and probably bound up, kept captive.

The police were uncaring at the beginning of the case, when she first reported it. They wouldn't be any better now. She even felt, at that point, that the police had something to do with Hilton's going missing. She had heard tales of police corruption before, but she never believed the stories. Not until now. The image of the mustached man flashed across her mind. Then it occurred to her, Zach and the police chief—they looked too similar! If they were relatives… Then it would surely be a different story. The police chief would want to shield Zach from the crimes that he committed …

She pressed a different number, fast.

There was a much better person to call…

CHAPTER TWENTY
PHONE CALLS

After a few moments of ringing, Dara answered.

"Ms. Meryl?" Dara seemed cheerful.

It was Ms. Meryl's turn. A brief silence passed, uncomfortable, almost timid. Then Ms. Meryl spoke.

"Hi there, Dara. Do you remember the case we were talking about two weeks ago? About my father? After my mother died? He is my only remaining family member, and I need your help."

"Absolutely! I do remember that one. What happened? Wait, do you want me to call up the other three girls first? The Case Devils? We can talk about the case again together. I can call you right back."

Dara's voice flushed with anticipation when she heard there was news about the case. The evening of their last meeting, two weeks ago, she had decided that the case was at a dead end. But now this new information brought it back to life again.

"Sure, thank you." Ms. Meryl said. And the call ended.

~   ~   ~

Dara called Sabrina. Her voice filled with a wave of excitement. Dara called Margaritte. Then she called Rachel.

Ms. Meryl sat on her sofa, contemplating. She tried playing easy games on her phone to distract her. She turned on the TV. But nothing seemed to be able to get Hilton's voice out of her mind.

Finally she took out her laptop from one of her office bags, and opened it. She searched for the name "Zach Cochlan"

The doorbell rang. Ms. Meryl shot up like a propeller launching, and went to the door.

The Case Devils— they were all there. Magaritte, Dara, Sabrina, and Rachel.

Ms. Meryl managed a slight smile for the girls, and led them inside to the living room. As soon as Fortinbras caught sight of the girls, he leaped up from his bed—more like a cushion—and threw himself on them. He pounced on Magaritte, forgetting that he was a 140 pound, huge Golden Retriever and Wolfhound mix. Magaritte, who was very light, would have fallen to the ground if Rachel hadn't caught her.

"Fort! Come down there! You'll hurt the girls, plus I'm in no mood for this today." Ms. Meryl called to Fortinbras, sternly, and held out her hand. Fortinbras, as if totally understanding what Ms. Meryl said, came to her immediately, and sat down obediently, wagging his tail. He stared his big, pleading eyes at Ms. Meryl, and blinked at her. Ms. Meryl shook her head and sighed. "No, no, no, Fort, not today."

She sat the girls down on the sofa and went into the kitchen to get them water to drink.

"So, what's the matter?" Sabrina was getting a bit impatient.

Ms. Meryl just sighed. She stood alone in the kitchen, and she kept pouring the cups of water silently from the pitcher of filtered water. She stared at the cupboard in front of her, for a bit too long. When she felt liquid on her hand, she jerked back into focus. The water had overflowed. It had trickled all the way down to the shelf underneath, and formed into a small puddle on the floor. Ms. Meryl stared numbly at the droplets of water, taking their time to move from the shelf edge to the floor. Her mind was blank.

"Ms. Meryl?" Rachel called out from the living room. The Case Devils were waiting.

Ms. Meryl was startled, but she hid it. Pushing her red glasses up her nose, she replied, "Oh, uh, hi." Quickly turning her back, she took the cups of water out for the girls. She placed them on the table in the living room.

"Girls, can you revisit the case we were discussing two weeks ago? Remember? The one about my missing father?" The girls nodded. Sabrina grabbed a cup and slurped from it, loudly.

"Well, my father called me. As you know, he has been missing for over one and a half months. Almost two now." Ms. Meryl replied, more quietly than usual, to hide the slightest quiver in her voice.

Sabrina stared wide-eyed at Ms. Meryl, almost coughing in astonishment. Dara raised an eyebrow, the famous DaraBrow. She was intrigued too.

"So what actually happened to him?" Rachel asked, also taking a cup from the table.

Ms. Meryl played the recording of her latest phone call. It started when she picked up the call that night.

"Look, if this is some annoying telemarketing, I'm suing you for selling my personal information." Ms. Meryl's voice was clear and crisp.

For a while, there was quiet on the other end of the phone. All the girls naturally leaned forward to try to hear a faint sound.

"Help…kidnap.." Hilton's whining was only barely audible from the background. Magaritte was the first to hear it. She gasped out loud, and said, in a whisper, "I think I can hear it!" The other girls heard it by then. "Oh, my goodness…" Dara said sharply; she was astonished.

"We can't know where he is exactly now, but the ID on the phone number he called me from shows he is outside Burlington, Vermont." Said Ms. Meryl.

"And where is that?" Sabrina asked innocently.

"Oh, Sabrina, we learned that in Geography class!" Rachel, the Geography expert, interrupted. "It's about a three hour drive from here."

"Good catch there," Dara smiled faintly.

Rachel sat on the couch beside Ms. Meryl, listening. Then she realized that Ms. Meryl had fallen asleep. Ms. Meryl's brain was so fatigued, she needed to rest.

Rachel motioned to the others and made a "shush" symbol with her finger. She walked over to Dara's side. The others noticed Ms. Meryl, curled up in the corner of the sofa. They tiptoed, with much care, to the other side of the living room, which led into the kitchen. They each took out their things from their bags—Magaritte a laptop, Dara a pen and a small notebook, Rachel a map of America that she ALWAYS brought with her just because she felt like it, and Sabrina a giant bottle of Simply Lemonade that she liked to drink.

They silently tiptoed again to the living room. Ms. Meryl was still sound asleep. Sabrina took Ms. Meryl's phone from the table, which still had the recording on it. The Case Devils gingerly stepped back into the kitchen. They closed the kitchen door silently behind them, to not disturb Ms. Meryl.

Dara hit the play button. Ms. Meryl's voice blasted out from the speaker, and it made everybody jump. In some way, it was funny. The stern Ms. Meryl's annoyed voice was so loud! They all tried to stifle down the laughs, but Sabrina broke out giggling, and suddenly everybody started giggling. Dara tried to shush everyone, though her eyebrows were still raised from laughing and she was choking on her own breath. A little while after, the girls settled down again and spoke in whispers when they realized that Ms. Meryl was still asleep on the couch. They stood there, frozen, staring at Ms. Meryl through the glass kitchen door. They were anxious to see if she had woken up. Ms. Meryl only stirred a little. She moaned quietly as she turned on her side. Her eyebrows were furrowed even though she was sleeping. The four girls sighed in tired relief that they had not woken her. They got back to work.

Lowering the volume, Dara played the recording again. Rachel was the first to make an inference: "Guys! I think I could hear an echo in the background when Hilton spoke."

Magaritte asked: "And where do you find echoes? If he was kidnapped, the kidnapper would likely put him in a hidden place, or at least where somebody outside couldn't see what's inside."

They dipped into silence.

Suddenly Sabrina thought of something. "The garage!" She said in a loud whisper. "There are echoes in the garage! And the garage is obscured with metal from the outside so nobody sees what's inside!"

Dara nodded, her eyes widening with satisfaction.

Sabrina was making an attempt to open her bottle of Simply Lemonade, but couldn't. She was trying so hard that her face was already a medium shade of red. Rachel noticed, and held out a hand: "Here, let me do it." Sabrina groaned as she suddenly released like a popped balloon, and handed the bottle to Rachel. Rachel spun it open easily by reversing direction, and winked when Sabrina's mouth dropped open with surprise.

All the while, Dara and Magaritte were having a fierce conversation.

"So…It's 1. Somewhere inside a big garage. 2. Near Burlington, Vermont. 3. In an extremely rural area." Magaritte summarized as she looked at her notes.

Dara nodded slightly. She reached out and talked to Rachel: "Can you plot it down? Like, specifically."

Rachel nodded. "Sure." She took out a pen from her bag and marked down two dots on the huge map of New England: Amherst, Massachusetts, and the area Hilton might be in now, Burlington, Vermont.

While they were all studying the map and locations, Sabrina just sat there, frowning and trying to make some sort of connection. Suddenly Sabrina stood up.

"Don't you guys think something is very wrong?" The three girls looked up at her simultaneously.

"What?" Dara asked.

Sabrina took a long breath. "Well…You see, she got a call from her FATHER. And her father has been gone for almost two months. But why didn't she call the police first? Why did she call us instead?"

They dipped into silence again.

"So," Sabrina continued, "I think that she has some conflict with the police. Or at least, had some encounter that caused her to not **TRUST** them." She bit hard on the word **TRUST**.

Dara thought for a while. "That does kinda make sense." She replied. "So if the case were like this, then we'll have to investigate the encounter first before we're able to make any—" She was cut off. Her cell phone rang.

"Oh guys, I think it's my mom." Dara said quietly, specifically to no one, but really to everyone. She held her watch to her ear, and through the silence, the other end of the phone could be heard faintly.

Her mom said: "Where have you been? Do you know how late it is now?" Her mom was upset. Yes, her mom was almost easily angered at anything.

Dara blushed and whispered back: " Um, mom, I'm at Sabrina's and I'll be home soon. I promise…" Everyone heard it. She had lied. Her mom sighed grumpily and ended the call.

"I certainly can't tell her that I'm at Ms. Meryl's house working on a mystery, can I?" She said quietly, to nobody, but more to give herself an excuse to lie. She looked more upset than usual.

They went silent for a while, not knowing what to say or how to say it.

Dara coughed and said quietly: "Let's continue with the case now, okay?"

The others nodded. And went silent again.

Again they were at a dead end. Just like two months ago.

Sabrina was the first to break the silence. "So, back to what I was talking about—"

Magaritte ended the sentence for her. "Ms. Meryl probably has some sort of strange conflict with the police agencies here—"

And Rachel added: "So that's why she called US instead of calling the police first?"

"Woah." Dara murmured. "That's a VERY big find."

Rachel drew a dotted line that connected the 2 points on the map.

"Well…If it's a 3 hour drive from here, that means if the kidnapper found out about us somehow, he would have enough time to get away, right?"

"I guess so…?" Sabrina said, her eyes still studying the map.

Magaritte was typing something on her laptop while they were discussing their theory. Everyone jumped when Magaritte suddenly stood up and raised her hands into the air in excitement. "Guys! Look at what I did!"

Sabrina poked her head around and stared at Magaritte's laptop. "What'd you do?" she asked with an innocent look on her face.

Magaritte, who was the absolute expert on coding, made a dramatic, shocked face at Sabrina.

"Don't you see? I cracked the ID code, so we can see **EXACTLY** where Hilton is now!"

The other girls stared at her blankly, not understanding what she just said.

"Uggh," Magaritte sighed, "So. Behind every ID code from a phone call, there is a map. The system locates the calls. But it's personal information, and unless you're some manager or boss of the phone company, you are unable to locate the call exactly. The ID written is just an imprecise description of where the caller was when the call was made. I COPIED the link of the ID area, and I literally broke into it."

Sabrina's mouth dropped open in awe.

"Woah. You must be some really fantastic hacker," she managed to say.

Magaritte smiled. "Nah, it's not really that hard, just that most people don't know how to do it." Magaritte answered quietly.

Dara's eyes brightened and she scrambled over to see what was on the computer. It was a map that looked similar to Google Maps, except that it was more detailed, and 3D. Magaritte double-clicked on her keyboard, and with the crisp sounds of the keys, a small red point appeared on the map. It marked exactly where Hilton should be now, or, at least where the phone was that Hilton used to make the call.

The girls just gazed in awe.

"That is **SO** cool." Dara said, almost in a whisper, without even taking her eyes off the laptop in Magaritte's hands. She reached out a hand and zoomed in on the map with two taps on the control area of the laptop. There was a small 3D diagram of the terrain and surrounding areas where Hilton might be.

"So that's where he IS now?" Sabrina asked, with an Oh-my-God-this-is-stupendous smile on her tanned face.

"Uh-huh." Magaritte replied, in response with a I-know-this-tone-is-ridiculous-but-I-wanna-be-cool-in-a-funny-way tone.

In the living room, Ms. Meryl moaned and stretched. The girls all looked in on her simultaneously, all holding their breath, afraid that

Ms. Meryl would wake up from their noise.

Rachel looked at her watch. It was 9:30pm. The fortunate thing was that it was a Friday.

Ms. Meryl woke up. She sat up slowly first before opening her eyes. She looked placid. At least, more comfortable than the days when she faced sleep disorders.

The girls just stared, then realizing that it wasn't quite polite to stare, turned back towards the computer again.

Suddenly they all jumped. Ms. Meryl's voice came from the living room, a bit flat from her sleep: "Dara? Sabrina? What are all you girls doing here?" She took a moment to reach and look at her phone for the time, before asking again: "What are you doing here? It's 9:30pm now? I mean, look, why would you guys even BE here at this point?"

The girls looked at each other, unsure what happened to Ms. Meryl. Sabrina whispered timidly under her breath: "I think she lost her memory temporarily or something."

Rachel shrugged. "At least she still KNOWS us, or she would have called the police, thinking it was an intruder!" Dara said quietly, afraid Ms. Meryl would be so astonished at their presence she would bellow at them: "I think she just slept too much. I don't think she has slept so soundly in a while." Magaritte, who had been silent while they whispered, now added: "We better explain to her what happened." The others nodded in approval.

Dara was the first to stand up and open the glass door, which, now they knew, wasn't very good at blocking sounds after all. The other girls followed close behind timidly, like little mice following some big leader mouse scurrying across the floor.

Ms. Meryl stared wide-eyed as the girls walked towards her.

Dara took a deep breath, using only eye-contact she motioned to the other girls to start talking... Well, the others didn't **QUITE**—at all—get the message! The girls dipped into silence for the billionth time that night. Dara was waiting for **THEM** to talk, and the girls were waiting for **DARA** to talk. They finally realized there was some kind of problem when nobody talked for at least an unbelievably long 30 seconds. Finally, Dara, showing her strong responsibility and leadership, found the nerve to talk first.

She sighed again before beginning. "Well, Ms. Meryl, you see, you might have lost part of your recent memory—temporarily." She added the word "temporarily" briskly and just in time, for Ms. Meryl was about to stand up and scream in fright, dramatically. Instead, Ms. Meryl sat down again and frowned at Dara. Dara stumbled a little, and blushed, "Um…So…Do you remember that your father Hilton went missing?" Ms. Meryl nodded, numbly.

Dara sighed. "Ugg…This is gonna get CONfusing." She murmured to herself, looking away at the others. "So, he was kidnapped, and that was the conclusion we came to together. Suddenly today Hilton called you, though it was not from HIS phone, but from an unknown number."

Ms. Meryl tilted her head slightly, and raised her knotted eyebrows together slowly as she stared at the bookshelf behind Dara. Her mind was wandering again. Ms. Meryl felt dizzy. The world around her was turning, and it was accelerating, accelerating, accelerating. The girl's faces were a mild blur, distorted out of shape. She felt an overwhelming force, as if from two gigantic hands, tuning her, stretching her like an elastic band, pushing her off a cliff. And she fell off. There was a sudden surge of weightlessness, like the climax of a rollercoaster.

Then everything went black. It wasn't exactly a black color. It was sort of a dark blankness, like it should have been day but with nothing inside the scene to fill the blank space up. Then Ms. Meryl came to the conclusion that she was still conscious. She started hearing things. Faint sounds from the background, as if from a different level of a different world, a wall of blankness dividing the two. And she was right in the middle of that boundary. She imagined drowning.

Ms. Meryl heard things more clearly now. The black blankness was still before her eyes. She could hear the familiar voices, and in a sudden pang in her mind she remembered everything. Sabrina. Dara. Rachel. Magaritte. Hilton's call. The phone number. The amulet. The events orbited around her head and spun like a carousel. The ideas went back and forth.

Suddenly she could hear. Her ears popped. The relief of air in her ears startled her, as did the voices of the girls that blasted into her ears. She tried to open her eyes, but her body was numb. She couldn't. She tried to open her croaked, dry mouth and tell the girls that she was okay, but couldn't do that either.

The girl's voices came from above; they were hovering over her. Dara was frantic: "What happened to her!" Magaritte was sobbing: "I don't know! I was just—"

With a surging force, Ms. Meryl suddenly opened her eyes and sat up. The girls stared with fear. And yes, Ms. Meryl remembered everything now. Her tongue hadn't totally recovered from that shock, and she was only able to quickly announce:

"GuysguysguysIamokayIreallyamokay." The girls weren't able to collect themselves, and Sabrina fell backwards in an instantaneous shock.

Dara, realizing what happened, sighed in relief.

"What happened to you?" she asked Ms. Meryl anxiously.

"We were about to call 911!" Sabrina almost yelled, she was so worried.

Ms. Meryl took a long breath.

"I'll go to check with my doctor tomorrow. Right now, I feel sort of okay."

Dara looked around. Rachel was in the kitchen, holding her laptop.

Ms. Meryl turned her head and tilted it slightly.

"What is this?" Ms. Meryl asked curiously, with a glint of hope in her eyes.

Rachel held the computer and coughed proudly.

"This is what we have achieved tonight! I was able to HACK into the GPS of the phone-call. "So **THIS**—" she pointed towards the red point on the laptop and used her fingers to zoom in, "—is exactly where Hilton used someone's phone to make the call."

Ms. Meryl dropped her mouth open in surprise. "Wow... That... Wow...That is stupendous."

Rachel smiled weakly, but the puny smile was filled to the brim with gratification. She was tired.

Dara's watch beeped. It was 9:40pm. She yawned and stretched back. She announced quietly: " Guys, I really think we should bicycle home."

Ms. Meryl suddenly reached out and grabbed her by the arm. "No." She said firmly. "You can't be alone at this hour. Please ask all of your parents to come and pick you up."

The sky was an almost opaque shape of dark blue, but the translucent clouds on the sky—a white, misty, unclear shadow—just proved that it was still translucent.

Rachel took her laptop and typed. Her typing was really fast, her fingers almost going around like a whirl. "There!" She clapped her hands together. "I sent you the link to the website, Ms. Meryl."

Ding! Went Ms. Meryl's phone, showing there was an email. Ms. Meryl smiled, a meaningful smile.

"I am so grateful," she said to them when they were all gathered in front of the door, "for the help all of you have given me, throughout the case. I don't think I would have been able to break it myself!"

The parents—annoyed moms, tired dads—all came to pick up each of the four girls. Magaritte and Sabrina went home together, as they lived just right next door.

Ms. Meryl waved at them. She climbed into the kitchen again and sat at the round table. She found a small paper note there, scrawled in Sabrina's handwriting. She frowned and read it slowly:

There is still one more thing I need you to tell me: WHY DIDN'T YOU CALL THE POLICE FIRST? Instead of us? what actually happened between you and the police?

Ms. Meryl took in a long breath and puffed it out slowly, feeling the slightly cool air with her lips. So… they had figured it out after all.

CHAPTER TWENTY-ONE
THE GARAGE

The garage was dark. Hilton was there, roped to the chair. It had almost been two and a half months since he was abducted. He only got food once a week. His lips were pale from starvation. The skin on his face was dry and cracked. The ends of his hair had turned from a bright silver, when he was just kidnapped, to a dull white that showed age. He seemed 10 years older than before he was taken.

Hilton's stomach ached. The last time he had a loaf of moldy bread was four days ago.

His throat was dry and sore, as if it had not been used in ages.

Zach came in. He smashed on the lights, which were not bright, but enough. Hilton's pale face was illuminated, and the light was blinding to Hilton after his eyes were accustomed to the darkness. After seeing Hilton there, Zach threw half a piece of moldy bread insultingly at Hilton's face, turned off the lights briskly again, and slammed the door behind him.

Something had dropped from his pocket. But Zach did not hear it.

Zach was more frustrated than ever. Last week's robbery failure messed things up. The amulet—he didn't get it! Someone had gotten it before he did, and the whole idea of that made him dig into his palm so hard with his nails he bled. He was still murmuring to himself when he came out of the garage.

Hilton held the piece of bread dearly, treasuring it in his hands. It was to be his food source for 3 days. He tore off one tiny piece, but before he was able to bring it to his mouth, he fainted. All he remembered seeing was pitch-darkness underneath his eyelids, not the type of dark he was used to in the garage. His mind was turned off, though he could still feel his consciousness faintly, and tried to open his eyes. He toppled over together with the chair he was tied to.

Zach sulked again outside for a while before moving away from the garage. Behind his angry face he was very nervous, for he was fully aware that Ms. Meryl would call the police the first thing in the morning if she noticed his arrival. Actually, though, Ms. Meryl did not, and that was beyond Zach's plan too. Zach still didn't fully face the fact that his plan was totally spiraling out of his control.

~   ~   ~

Hilton opened his eyes and blinked. He did not know the time. There were no windows in the garage. A mouse scrambled over the floor, making small scratching sounds.

Hilton got up painfully, straining every muscle. He sat straight, then toppled again. Sat straight and toppled again. He seemed to repeat this forever, then he finally sat up straight.

He looked around. Just the same old environment. He just sat there, transitioning between dreams and reality.

Hilton was just about to drift into sleep again when there was a dinging sound. It seemed sharper than ever in the silent garage. Hilton forced himself to sleep again. The dinging sound continued. He opened his eyes properly. A pulse of light illuminated part of the dusty garage ceiling. It happened again. Hilton peered over, trying to see what was there. He squinted. The brightness of the light source contrasted sharply with the dark surroundings.

Finally Hilton was able to see the light source clearly. He held back a gasp.

A phone.

Zach's phone.

For the almost four months he had been kidnapped and kept in this 'picturesque' place, this was the first sign of hope Hilton saw. Not just hope. Freedom.

He nudged his feet against the ground and moved forward towards the phone, dragging along the chair he was tied to. The little distance had cost him much effort. He kept pushing...

Hilton was about halfway through when suddenly his ankle hit the ground. He groaned lightly in frustration. He had sprained it.

At first there was no pain, just a deadened sensation. Hilton was about to try to move forward again when suddenly an overwhelming wave of pain surged across him. It was like having cold water poured on him.

Hilton, losing his balance, fell forward. He hit the ground hard. The pain was overwhelming. Hilton was on the verge of losing consciousness again. But then he awakened again. He gritted his teeth to overcome the pain. Now it was a hot, throbbing feeling on his ankle. By now it had become swollen and big. He nudged along the ground, bit by bit. Huge beads of sweat had formed on his brow.

After a period of time that seemed like forever, Hilton was near the phone. The ground was dusty and messy with cobwebs. Under the cobwebs were tools that seemed to have been in the garage forever. His eyes searched around for tools that could cut his rope. Then he found it. A small knife. His hands were tied but his arms were free. He carefully held the end of the knife in his mouth and sawed his hands against the blade._Slowly but steadily, he used the knife to cut through the rope that tied his hands. The rope finally broke. A faint smile jumped to Hilton's mouth. He realized Zach had been careless when he tied him up.

Hilton's hands were now free, and they were purple and swollen. The rope had been tight indeed. But Hilton didn't care all that much. As much as his hands felt numb after being tied for so long, he was anxious to get the phone.

Hilton reached out and held the phone, struggling to keep it steady as his hands trembled. He quickly tried to open it. There was a passcode. Hilton could not hide the despair in his eyes. In his anger, he typed random numbers on the passcode. They were wrong. He was flooded with fury. He kept typing in random numbers, hitting the screen hard. Then the phone shut down. He had tried too many times. On the screen were the big words: 'Your attempts have been too frequent. Please try again after 15 minutes.'

Hilton wanted to smash the phone on the ground. He wanted it to break into a thousand pieces. But he recovered his rational thinking. The hand holding the phone, about to smash it, hung in midair. Then he sighed, and put his arm down again.

"No way," He murmured under his breath. He felt like a tiger in a cage. Roaring. But not able to gain its freedom. The metal bars were sturdy.

Hilton waited. It seemed to take forever. After infinite scratching sounds made by scuttling mice and the dripping sounds of leaking droplets of water from pipes, the phone finally refreshed again.

Hilton held it tightly. He recovered his reason for trying. He thought properly. He typed in Zach's birthday. He knew his birthday. They had been friends. But that was a long time ago. Before things started going all wrong. Wrong. Really wrong. The passcode was wrong too. Hilton thought again. His brain felt like it was spinning. But he steadied it. He trembled slightly. For a moment he seemed like he was going to topple over, to faint, but he came back to attention. He typed the last six numbers in Zach's phone number. Wrong. Hilton raised a hand to wipe the thin layer of sweat on his forehead. He breathed in heavily. One last chance. He typed in Zach's mother's birthday. Zach had always spoken with love about his mother. The passcode worked.

The phone unlocked. A blinding light from the screen forced Hilton to shut his eyes. After a few moments he opened them again and blinked furiously to get used to the light. Then he touched the screen and dialed Ms. Meryl's phone number. He pressed the green button and called. He was tense now. This was survival or death. He waited. After a few seconds, the sound of ringing came from the phone. It blasted out at top volume. Hilton, startled, jumped with his chair. He quickly turned the speaker phone off, he hadn't realized it was on. He prayed that Zach did not hear him.

Then Ms. Meryl answered. Hilton's pulse quickened. He was about to say something when he was knocked out again by sheer fatigue. Ms. Meryl's voice, despite the low volume, echoed faintly in the garage.

"Hello?" Hilton could hear her, but could not move. His body seemed numb and wouldn't listen to his instructions.

"Hello?" She said again, this time a bit louder. Hilton was anxious now. He wanted to hold the phone up and reply, but…He just couldn't move. He tried desperately to lift his arm, but it was sore and numb. Her voice, now angry and a bit raspy, came from the other end again. "Look, I don't know this number, if this is some kind of annoying telemarketing I'm suing you for selling my personal information." Hilton could not use his voice. He wanted to tell her what happened to him, where he was, his condition, but no, no reaction came from him. He was wide awake, conscious, but his eyes were closed.

~   ~   ~

Upstairs, Zach was drowsy. So much had happened over the past few months that sometimes he couldn't even catch up with what was happening. He slipped into his pajamas, and into bed. The room was dim. What Zach did not notice was his phone was missing…

~   ~   ~

Hilton woke up again. He felt a long time had passed since he was knocked out, but he realized it had only been 40 minutes when he looked at the phone. He unlocked it again, this time with confidence, and dialed Ms. Meryl's number. She answered after a few brisk moments. Her voice was reluctant.

"Again?" Hilton could hear her murmur under her breath. He croaked out, word by word, pain in his voice with every sound he made.

"Elizabeth…Save me...Kidnapped…" Some words he made were even unidentifiable to himself. Ms. Meryl gasped. Hilton felt his heart caught in his throat from all the anticipation and excitement. He didn't talk any more. Just the simple movements had taken away all the energy he had. He used the very last bit to end the call and delete the traces. Then he slept, or blacked out, he did not know.

CHAPTER TWENTY-TWO
ZACH'S STORY

Zach woke up. His room felt no different despite the bright sun outside. The curtains were always drawn. The dim lamp was always lit. It was a gloomy room, that stayed in the messy, careless way all four seasons of the year, and was shrouded by dust. Zach never even thought to open the curtains and let in the bloom of the sun. He might be seen, and he didn't like it.

He felt for his phone. It should be at the corner of the table next to the bed—no. Zach frowned. He didn't feel his phone. He flipped around the blanket anxiously. He raised the whole blanket. The phone. It was not there.

He climbed off the bed and stood up. He was frowning now, his eyebrows so curved they almost tied into a knot. He thought, resting his chin on his hand unconsciously. He remembered yesterday night he had fallen into bed and dozed off without trying to find anything, or even, ensure the presence of his phone. At no point had he considered that Hilton was holding the phone right now, typing into it, raising his hand wanting to break it, but lowering it again in the consideration that this was his only source of mild hope.

Zach stared at the wall clock. It was 9:30 in the morning. He was frustrated. He felt dizzy. His stomach was getting the better of him, and he stood there for a small while, leaning back against his bedroom wall and closing his eyes. He needed to refresh with a meal, his head was spinning now. He went downstairs. Barefoot. He didn't notice the cold. He was used to it. There were times, when he was little, that he and his mother would have to sleep out on the streets, hopelessly, fading into the cold. They had been homeless, and it wasn't just one or two times. It happened almost every time his mother changed boyfriends, always ending it with some kind of argument then being escorted out the door. The worst time it happened he was wearing only pajamas, and it was snowing outside. He had a fever that winter. The only dwelling he and his mother had sort of "owned" that winter had been a huge cardboard box. But his mother had always tried to make the best of things, even in the worst of times. She had been snappy, sometimes, yes, but she was able to sort everything out.

Thinking over it now, Zach realized that she was as cold as he was that winter. But she had made everything all right again. By herself. When he was just born, he lived on this beautiful farm surrounded by daffodil fields with his mother and father. Then his father died, when Zach was only two, and things had never been the same again. Zach could only remember pieces of this time, he knew about the daffodils from his mother.

Zach's mother was the rightful owner of the house. But then one night he heard people coming into the house, hordes of people, and he was really scared. He hid in his bedroom. He remembered hearing his mother, shouting at the people. Then it was all silent again. At midnight, his mother came upstairs to find him, and he first saw his mother so fragile, tear-streaked. He asked through gurgled baby words what was going on. But his mother didn't answer. And so he never knew. His mother just silently started packing his things up. When he saw this house again, 15 years later, it had a middle-aged couple living in it. He and his mother were on their way to the train station to find his uncle after being thrown out again. He had just one moment while his mother was fussing with their luggage, and not knowing anything at the time, he stepped in front of the house and rang the bell. The Man, probably in his fifties at the time, answered the door.

"Why are you living in my house?" Zach asked confidently, with a touch of arrogance. The Man chuckled patiently.

"Why, young lad, I thought we had bought this house." The

middle aged man had stood his ground.

"Well, I think you are mistaken. I lived in this house with my mother and father before. " Zach said.

The Man smiled.

"Well, well, well, I have finally found the rightful owner of the house! As you see, it's a long story…"

"Zach!" His mother had called, interrupting the conversation. "Get your legs moving! We're gonna be late for the train!"

His mother grabbed his arm and hauled him away to the station. He didn't learn about the story until over a decade later.

In his 30s, Zach returned to the old house again. The same man, with the exact same features, answered the door. The Man was elderly now, and he had kept a huge Golden Retriever and Wolfhound mix. He seemed to faintly remember Zach.

"Is it you again?" He asked playfully.

"Yes, sir." Zach answered brightly. Then, from inside the house, a massive golden dog rushed out and almost pushed Zach down. Zach ruffled the dog's fur and the golden monster painted back, almost smiling in satisfaction.

"What's his name?" Zach asked the elderly man with a child-like, innocent look on his face.

"Ah…we have named him Fortinbras, but as he is my dog I like personally calling him 'Old Fort.'" The old man chuckled as he replied slowly.

Zach reached out for the jackets laid on the small table next to the kitchen, feeling for his phone inside, but he did not feel the hard, black rectangle. Zach was quite frantic now that his phone was missing. He was frowning so hard that his mind ached and sweat gathered on his forehead. He stared into the area of empty space, as if searching for his phone in the past. He remembered…giving Hilton a piece of bread, and sulking in the hallways, and then retiring to bed. Suddenly he lit up. Yes…the garage, that's where the phone must be!

Zach dashed downstairs. Hilton was still unconscious. Before he passed out, Hilton had tossed Zach's phone far enough away that Zach would not be suspicious.

Zach threw the door open, and the sudden light was blinding. Even still in a faint, Hilton was able to feel the change in his surroundings. Zach saw the phone. He cast a blind eye to the fainted Hilton, who was weak with white lips, and tied to the chair. He was pale, almost like a ghost, and was now so skinny that at one glance you would feel he was no flesh but solely bone.

Hilton woke up, but did not dare to open his eyes yet. He felt Zach's cold glance at him and the blinding, white light from outside the garage stinging his eyes. Zach picked up the phone. He unlocked it and checked for any suspicious records. There weren't any, since Hilton had deleted them all. The phone looked perfectly normal. So he left.

Hilton was left in the darkness, the type he had been used to for already two months. But he smiled. Help would hopefully be arriving soon.

CHAPTER TWENTY-THREE
PONDERING

Ms. Meryl asked in the front seat, "Is everyone buckled in?" There was a cold glint of anger to her usually soft eyes.

"Yes," came the solemn reply from the four usually energetic kids. They were excited, every one of those hearts pounding rapidly. But they hid it under their sober faces. They knew this was no adventure. At least for Ms. Meryl.

"Last call for the bathroom. This is going to be an over 3 hour drive–it's about 200 miles, but I'm all gassed up, we will not stop. That means no bathroom breaks." Ms. Meryl spoke very fast. She felt, yes, she felt it clearly. She was going to find Hilton today. She had used the website Magaritte found out about. She had done research. It was a game of time.

"Yes," the simultaneous answer came again. Sabrina had all the evidence of Hilton's actions printed out, in a folder. Dara stayed alert in her seat, trying to resist her nausea from the car ride. Magaritte was trying her best to swallow her anticipation, because it always came back to her throat. She had never seen Hilton before. None of them had. They knew this journey wasn't safe, not exactly. But they each had their own plans to fight for survival, if any danger did come. Rachel wasn't in the best of moods today, despite this massive incident they were now heading into. Sabrina kept fumbling over the sheets of evidence she had in the folder and her notes. They DID know where Hilton was now, and hopefully they would find him, but she still wanted to know the whole story…how Hilton slipped into so much debt in merely a few months. How the amulet came to be gone. How, later, as Ms. Meryl had told them, she found the amulet broken in the theater. How Hilton was likely a gambler now. How Hilton had also used an unknown number to call them, likely on the kidnapper's phone... But most of all, Sabrina wanted to know why Ms. Meryl did not call the police to report it when she got the call from Hilton!

Sabrina sat pondering in her seat. The minivan was hot, and she was sweating. She felt dizzy. All of the events spun around rapidly in her head. She took out her little notebook and drew a small storyline in it. At the beginning she wrote: "Hilton is a gambler" and at the end she wrote: "Ms. Meryl calls the Case Devils."

Suddenly Sabrina remembered something. The phone call. The detention she had a long time ago. She heard——Ms. Meryl arguing on the phone! And the same ringtone later when she came to her house for a parent meeting! That was probably the police, that Ms. Meryl had been so nervous about when Sabrina asked her. And—Ms. Meryl DID tell them once about her hate for the police! That time the Case Devils were having a "conference" at her house and they rode their bikes to a cafe. That was when SHE saw Ms. Meryl. Ms. Meryl told her, after they all went, that she didn't like the police. Sabrina couldn't remember something…when the familiar voice rang in her head: "Ugh, that abominable mustached man! I do remember… he was sort of tanned, and had a VERY annoying, curled mustache. He didn't research my father's case AT ALL. Plus he does look like a mouse!" Now she remembered what Ms. Meryl said. The mustached man. Hmm. Interesting.

Sabrina's thoughts were cut off for a second. She just…ran out of thoughts. Mindlessly, she flipped through the plastic folder again. It popped open. Sabrina sighed. "Oh, bad quality. I guess I've really seen enough of those." She threw it on the seat next to her, which was the only empty one in the minivan. The other girls filled the rest. After all, it wasn't really a "minivan"—only a car with a max capacity of six. Adding Ms. Meryl in they had five people already. Sabrina's thoughts were wandering until they landed firmly…on a chocolate milkshake. She shook her head and punished herself. Is this really the time to be milk-shaky? Ugg. Sabrina was sweating. Ms. Meryl DID promise AC in the car, didn't she? Well I guess then the car is WAY too old, because this AC was hot! Sabrina had already taken off the jacket her mother had insisted on her wearing, it was unhelpful in this sudden heatwave. So, Sabrina could only blame it on the inaccurate—if not totally off—weather prediction.

Sabrina found a small piece of paper in the folder. It was ripped off from one of the other notebooks she had at home. She turned it around and read her own scribbled writing:

"March 4th.

Ms. Meryl told me she saw one of Hilton's friends before. Hmm. Maybe it isn't totally relevant, but I'll note it anyway. So. Basically she was at Hilton's, collecting old books he didn't want, and he was watching a game with his friends at that big house of his. She said The Man looked similar to one of the police officers at the station. That's quite a coincidence, isn't it, that her father's friend actually looked similar to the police chief? The Man was tanned and had a thin mustache. He was called Zach; very grayish–colored eyes, and they were deep-set. She also told me The Man had black hair. I've got nothing else to tell."

Sabrina's eyes widened. Tanned face. Mustache. Were they…biologically related? They **JUST** studied that in Ms. Meryl's biology class! That you could look more like your relatives preceding you rather than your parents because of trait variation! Hmm. Maybe she didn't remember it totally correctly, but still…She thumped her hand on her lap. This was way too coincidental. She couldn't believe it. She stamped the thought firmly into her head and noted it as a side point on the little notebook in her lap. "Hilton's friend, Zach, might have been biologically related to the police chief here. The police chief would NOT accept Ms. Meryl's case about Hilton, and refused to investigate it further."

Noticing how she forgot something, she quickly added a new bullet point:

"Ms. Meryl hates the police chief (and the whole police system here)."

Sabrina's jacket was in her lap. It was humid in the car, and she saw that the other girls were sweating too. Ms. Meryl was also sweating, but not that much. Sabrina gazed for a brief second. Ms. Meryl was driving intently, yet the eyes reflected in the rear-view-mirror seemed hollow. Her brows were knitted together. She wasn't speaking or joking lightly like she normally would. Tension was in the air, together with all the gloominess and humidity of the car.

Sabrina tilted her head a little and went back to analyzing. She held a printout of Hilton's spending report from his bank account, and was frowning at it without noticing that she frowned.

Why would **ANYONE** need so much money all at once? Sabrina asked again, though she kept her answer in her heart: he was a gambler, of course! And he probably lost, like, really badly. Hilton most likely didn't want to trouble Ms. Meryl, so he borrowed lots of money from other people. She scanned the paper more closely. At the very bottom there was a line showing the debt.

"January…$200,000…Owed to Zachary Cochlan."

Sabrina frowned, then dropped her mouth open in astonishment. So all the debts Hilton had owed…they were to his friend Zach! And looking at the chart now, Hilton still hadn't been able to return the debts.

Now, for the amulet issue. Sabrina remembered Ms. Meryl bringing them to Hilton's house, and trying to find the amulet one night. But it seemed to be lost. Then Ms. Meryl had found it in the **CINEMA** when she went to watch a movie some weeks after.

Sabrina was really frustrated now. All she had worked out were mere guesses, possibilities. There was a slight possibility that maybe, just maybe, Hilton owed a lot of money to Zach. Zach needed the money back now, but Hilton wasn't able to return it. So, Zach kidnapped him, AND the police chief was his relative and shielded him by not pursuing the case.

She dozed off. Her heart was thumping. They were going to come face to face with the kidnapper.

CHAPTER TWENTY-FOUR
RESCUE

The drive was very long. Soon Rachel and Sabrina were dozing off. Dara was trying to cool down from the heat by sticking her face on the glass window, which, disappointingly, was as hot as a stove too. Magaritte was reading a novel she had brought. None of them seemed to be excited, but their hearts were burning under their placid exteriors. Part of it, though, was that they knew it was sort of dangerous, but that also made it fun.

It was three hours of tedious driving. Ms. Meryl was still hollow though intently focused on the driving, and occasionally beeped impatiently at the timidly slow drivers on the highway in front of her. She was a careful driver though, and intent on keeping the girls as safe as possible.

They had already been on their drive for two and a half hours. The terrain was changing. There was a dark trash bag on one side and it wavered around in the wind, like a clawing hand in the air.

Sabrina woke up. Her head was aching, and her neck was in pain.

She couldn't move her head. Her position when sleeping was bad. Like, really bad. Part of her neck was squashed and part of it was strained.

"This is the best thing ever!" Sabrina groaned lightly in a sarcastic way as she attempted to slowly move her head. She moaned. But she used her left hand and abruptly hit her head into position. Her neck was STILL very sore.

Ms. Meryl sighed heavily. The girls could feel her fear too. But the smell of fear lingered in the air for a while then moved on. Ms. Meryl's eyebrows were tied together. They were arriving at an area that was very dirty, and rubbish was scattered all over the place: soda cans, plastic bags, water bottles, so many it seemed almost like a trash dump. The road split into 2 paths. The GPS was telling Ms. Meryl to turn left. But she took a deep breath and stepped hard on the accelerator and spun the wheel. They turned right.

The girls inhaled in shock. Dara was bold enough: "Umm…Ms. Meryl, did you…umm…go in the wrong direction?" She was timid and stumbled over her words, because Ms. Meryl's face had such a dark, moody shade to it Dara didn't dare speak any more.

Ms. Meryl cleared her voice. She hadn't spoken once throughout the nearly three hour drive. Her voice was raspy at first, but she coughed lightly a few times and it went back to the stern, clear voice: "Yes, I did."

The girls were both confused and a bit scared. What should they do now? Would they…get lost? Why did Ms. Meryl turn right even if she KNEW that they should turn left?

They went quiet for a while. And for God's sake, the air conditioning of the minivan finally decided to behave itself for the last 20 minutes. That was some bitter delayed comfort, though, for the girls. They had been sweltering in the heat and humidity of the car the whole time.

~ ~ ~

Hilton was pale. He was famished. Each second felt like ages. He barely ever spoke, almost never, in his 4 months of abduction, except for the times when Zach hit him and he moaned. He stared into blank space. His voice was raspy, his throat so dry his voice sounded non-human. He needed water. Zach insulted him by putting his tiny amount of water in a bucket that he also used to feed pigs. And Hilton had to drink from it by leaning down, which was painful for him tied to a chair. He would have to fall on his knees on the cold, hard stone floor. He would have to bear the excruciating pain while contorting himself into a strange position. Only then he could barely reach the cool water. The water was dirty too, almost murky.

The moldy bread Zach had thrown on his face two days ago had run out a long time ago. At least, it seemed like a long time for Hilton because he was so hungry. He coughed. His stomach churned with hunger. He would do anything now, even for a tiny piece of bread. Even if it was moldy. And thrown on his face.

He lost his balance on the chair. He felt dizzy. He tipped to one side. He fell with the chair.

Hilton fainted. His last thoughts were still counting down the hours till help would come.

~   ~   ~

Ms. Meryl kept driving. They circled around the kidnapper's home and parked down in an area where they were directly behind the house on the GPS system Magaritte hacked into. Nobody from the outside would be able to see them.

Ms. Meryl said slowly, biting on each word: "We. Have. Arrived." The girls unpacked themselves and loaded their camouflage coats. Sabrina and Rachel would be hiding in bushes far from the house, and observe the kidnapper's actions or where he went to with binoculars. Dara was going to place an electric lock at both the main gate and the back door so the kidnapper wouldn't escape when Ms. Meryl commanded.

Ms. Meryl checked her watch. The sky was dimming.

Ms. Meryl climbed into a window of the house. Her heart was

beating really fast.

She opened the window using a strong wire and cocked it open from underneath. She climbed in. There was a whisper in her headphones. It was Sabrina's voice: "Ms. Meryl, the kidnapper is in his room. I saw him turn on the lights just now. Second floor."

Ms. Meryl inhaled heavily. She was at the first floor. It was dark. She felt her way into the main living room. There was rubbish scattered on the carpet, and she tried to make it past it as quietly as possible. She was about to reach the staircase that lead to the underground level. The garage. Where. Hilton. Was. Kept. She was angry now. At the kidnapper. At Hilton himself. She wasn't even afraid if the kidnapper found her. She just wasn't.

She hit a tin can. Clack. Thump. Bang. Apparently she had kicked it with some force, because it rolled over a distance and hit the wall again. She heard footsteps.

She climbed rapidly behind the drawn curtains near the window as noiselessly as possible. And she hid there. The footsteps neared. The light turned on. She held her breath.

~   ~   ~

CHAPTER TWENTY-FIVE
REUNITED

The footsteps headed for the kitchen. Ms. Meryl closed her breath and prayed. But the suspected kidnapper only took something from the refrigerator and headed upstairs again. He had not noticed Ms. Meryl. She sighed in relief. Ms. Meryl was kneeling behind the curtain, and her knees were sore. She scrambled out and headed directly for the underground garage. The garage was big, and a heavy metal door led to it. Ms. Meryl turned the wheel and the metal door opened, squeaking unwillingly at the hinges. She froze. For a second she thought the kidnapper spotted her.

She whispered into her headphones, so quietly even a mouse wouldn't be able to hear: "Where is he now?"

Rachel's reassuring voice came back, quiet too: "In his room still. We'll tell you if he makes any moves downstairs."

"Sure." Ms. Meryl exhaled a little. She had been holding her breath.

She went down the narrow, short staircase that led to the garage.

The garage door. Was. Locked. Ms. Meryl sighed and knotted her eyebrows. Sweat was collecting on them. She wiped them briskly. Sweat was blurring her eyes. She pulled out a pair of small knives from her bag. She stuck one end of the blunted knife in the lock and turned the entirety of the huge lock. It wouldn't budge. She held her breath and pressed harder. Her hands were burning, red from the forcefulness. At last the huge lock turned a little. She pressed more.

It was hard. But she opened it. She couldn't describe the overwhelming feeling when the lock finally opened with a click. She gingerly pulled open the door of the garage.

Hilton heard it. He heard the spinning in front of the door. And the click. His heart was beating fast. Was it Zach coming to torment him, or even to kill him? Or was it someone coming to help? He did not know. So he waited anxiously.

Ms. Meryl saw the chair in the middle of the room. She watched for a second, not even realizing that it was Hilton. The figure tied to it…was so pale, so skinny, as if there were no flesh on his whole body. It was not like Hilton. But then Ms. Meryl saw his face. It had to be Hilton, even if he did not look like the man he had been two months ago.

"Dad," she whispered.

"I'm sorry," he said.

"No time now, we'll talk later," she said.

And then they were both quiet, focused on his ropes.

Ms. Meryl brought out a knife. This time a sharp one. She edged forward quietly and sawed open the thick bundles of rope that were binding Hilton to the chair. In the garage was only the sound of thin slashing on the rough ropes and Hilton's heart, beating.

The last strand of rope broke. Ms. Meryl held Hilton up, but the moment he stood up, he fell to the ground again. With a loud thud. Both of them froze. He had been sitting for too long.

Zach heard it.

Ms. Meryl didn't think. She held Hilton and carried him on her back. He was much lighter than she thought he would be. She lunged across the large, cold garage. To the other side. There was a window there. She could break it and leave.

There were footsteps from upstairs. They were loud, every step landing firmly on Ms. Meryl's heart. She was beyond panic now. She ran on instinct. Her innate will found a way through desperation.

The footsteps were nearing. She could hear Zach raising the huge metal lock.

She smashed her free hand into the window. The window was higher up in the garage than she thought. But she would be able to climb it.

The creaking door to the garage. It was opening. Behind her back she would be able to feel the light crawling in rapidly. Then a shadow loomed over.

She was already reaching the window. She pulled. Her weak, untrained muscles pulled. Pulled with all they had, focused on their single will for survival.

"Stop right there!" There was a deep, man's voice. Then came a clanging on the floor from metal. A dagger, probably.

She sprinted, so fast her legs were numb to the speed.

Then nothing.

She did not know where she was. She felt Hilton's weak breath behind her.

She was on wet grass. They were through.

She stood up. She lifted Hilton up and carried him again.

Zach had not followed them up. They were in the back garden.

She was tired. Her heartbeat was getting slower. She made her torn leg muscles walk all the way to where their minivan was parked. She put Hilton in the backseat.

The Case Devils were overflowing with questions.

"Where is he?"

"Is he okay?"

"What about the kidnapper?"

"What do we do now?"

Ms. Meryl waved them away.

"What happened to your hand?" Sabrina's shrill voice cut through everyone else's.

Ms. Meryl was about to close her eyes. Then she opened them again and looked down at her hands. The right one, which she had smashed the glass window with, was bloody. Broken pieces of glass cut right into her flesh. It had felt painless before; now the pain was surging through her, like massive but silent waves that would drown her will and grit in one slap of the cold, blue water.

Sabrina acted first. She drew out their medical kit from the back of the minivan. She took out disinfectant and bandages. She cleaned the wound and bandaged the fingers. "You must go to the hospital. ASAP."

Ms. Meryl smiled a little. At Sabrina's rarely serious face.

She reached out a hand, as if asking for something, but really just to see her own bloody hands in the dim moonlight. She asked while not taking her eyes off the Case Devils: "Did you guys do as I said?" She was smiling through her pulsing pain, as if she was confident with what their answer would be.

They nodded.

"Yes. We locked his front and back yard."

"I secured all the windows. And I actually had to put a board behind so he wouldn't be able to break it."

"Great. Call the police now. You can talk." Ms. Meryl lay in the back of the minivan and closed her eyes. She was listening to the other world. The world with only insects and grass and the dew from the tips of grass.

The girls called the police. Not the biased, local ones. They called the FBI to report an interstate kidnapping. Now solved.

~   ~   ~

Silence. After so much hard work they hadn't even had time to think of what they had done and rejoice. Ms. Meryl went to the front of the car. Hilton was sitting there, in the passenger's seat. His eyes were closed. Sleeping. Ms. Meryl's feelings were complicated. Somewhat beyond words. But mostly she was feeling happiness. An overwhelming happiness. Hilton opened his eyes slightly and slowly. Ms. Meryl hugged him. They had not seen each other for two months, even more than that, and each second now they felt in constant fear that they would lose one another. But now they were together again, and they each swore in their hearts that they would never be separated again. Never.

The FBI, police and emergency services arrived. Not with blaring sirens and lights, but silently. There were about eight of them, two of them women doctors, two male FBI agents, and four strong police officers. One of the police officers was a woman. She was tanned, and very tall. The familiar features alerted Ms. Meryl. Tanned. Grey eyes! Ms. Meryl sat up now. No! There was something not right about this policewoman! She might be connected to the kidnapper! Ms. Meryl's breath grew raspy. They were everywhere. She had only known what the kidnapper looked like from her predictions, that the kidnapper was related to Zach Cochlan and based on what Zach Cochlan looked like. It was all…built on a tower of hypothesis, each layer stacking harder and heavier than the last. But better to be sure than leave a tiger out in the wild.

Ms. Meryl had sat up by now. Her blue eyes had a silvery, cold glint to them. She was very suspicious.

"Where is he?" The policewoman asked. Ms. Meryl did not answer. She stared into the eyes of the policewoman.

"Can you show me your badge?" Ms. Meryl inquired.

The policewoman showed her. It read, in huge bold letters: Mary Cochlan.

"The kidnapper's last name is Cochlan." Sabrina cut in.

"Are you biologically related to Zach Cochlan?" Ms. Meryl asked.

The policewoman frowned. "That is beyond this investigation, ma'am."

The policewoman was annoyed by now.

Three other officers were watching. The tallest one cut in now, a bit of his self-dignity mixed with an impatient mind: "Ma'am," he addressed Ms. Meryl, "if you think it absolutely vital that Mrs. Cochlan be excluded from this action we will accept that for now. But it is our priority to arrest the kidnapper."

Ms. Meryl nodded. "Alright, as long as SHE stays out of it, I'm fine with anything."

They found Zach sitting right behind the front door. Sabrina and the girls had locked it from the outside with a huge lock, and he couldn't escape. Trapped like a bee in a bear's mouth, that's what they say.

The police arrested him solemnly. He didn't make any gestures to show resistance. He just followed them down to where their car was and stayed there, in their car. His eyes were very hollow. It was like his spirit was just dragged out of them. He wouldn't blink, staring mindlessly into the air. His colored eyes were now full of blood vessels. They were sort of creepy, in a way. He was blank.

The police left. The policewoman glared at Ms. Meryl. The police were holding Zach and bringing him to his car.

Ms. Meryl smiled back.

Hilton's chest heaved. He sat up now. Rubbed his eyes as if there was a whole well in them. Stared at Ms. Meryl in disbelief. Stared at the girls more in disbelief.

The Case Devils, Ms. Meryl and Hilton left to wash up and get to sleep. Processing the crime scene took hours. The night air felt fresh with the tingling of eager dawn.

CHAPTER TWENTY-SIX
CASE SOLVED

It was mid day, weeks later. The four girls were in fresh, vibrant clothes. Youth beamed from their faces, each distinct. It was in the air: their powers, their strength, their energy, their infinite potential. Sabrina was in a bright Barbie-pink shirt (it was summer) and pink jeans. She was eager to share what she figured out of the case with the press, and this is the one interview they all agreed to do.

Ms. Meryl was formal, and stern, like she always used to be. She was sitting at the other end of the long meeting table. Hilton was next to her. Some color had returned to his face, and he had gained some weight that he was not totally bones now. But his eyes still looked weary, without life, just a cloudy blue, and his face was the best evidence, still, for sleep fatigue. Dark bags hung from his eyes. His eyes were still a crystal blue color, yet many of their twinkles were worn down and polished out from his life. The lines on his brow had thickened, and they were dark, deep lines that seemed to be carved into his old face. It was only more than three months, but he had aged like it was years. But the wrinkles that were once next to his eyes had thinned, because he smiled less, and wasn't as careless as before.

The interviewer was mostly asking questions to Hilton and Zach, who was out on bail awaiting trial.

"Lay the whole story out."

Zach breathed in. He was empty. He needed no one now.

"Hilton is a gambler." Though he seemed initially placid in his own careless way, a rising fury could be felt in the shake of his voice at the word "gambler." He swallowed the anger raw. He was back to that spiritless, drowning placidity again.

Hilton wasn't really surprised. He knew Zach so well, he would predict that would be the first thing Zach would say. Zach was not the kind of person that would lay ALL of his faults in front of you, even once you discovered his lies. You would have to pop every truth yourself. He was not going to feed you the information.

Magaritte stifled a yawn. The interviewers were quite monotonous. The Man kept staring at the coffee mug in front of him, and the woman would shoot him a look that made him go back to spinning his pen on his notepad again. The woman sort of half-sighed, then continued down the list the police detective had handed her. Magaritte tried to focus on the story. Yes, he's a gambler. Yes, he lost a lot of money. Her eyes were drooping. Then she suddenly jerked up by a small but penetrating pain in her left leg. She jumped a little, starting Rachel, who was to the right of her. Embarrassed a little, she looked around to see if anyone else had seen what happened.

Nobody seemed to notice except from a curious raise of the eyebrows from Rachel. Magaritte turned left and faced a mischievous Sabrina, who had just pinched her on the leg to keep her from falling asleep. Sabrina was hiding her mouth with her hand now, so the others wouldn't see her curving mouth. Magaritte harrumphed a little when she realized Sabrina just saw her jump, then smiled a little as she played the scene again in her mind. But she still glared at Sabrina for a millisecond, and Sabrina caught it. Magaritte shrugged, and Sabrina's little hand-wave, as if brushing the matter aside, revealed that Magaritte was falling asleep. Sabrina pinched her to wake her up.

Zach was speaking now. Sabrina nudged Magaritte, reminding her to listen. Magaritte nodded slightly and cast a fast glimpse at Sabrina giving her the okay-okay-okay-I-get-it-fine-you-just-want to-end-my-fun grin Magaritte-special-look. Sabrina curled her mouth, but was shielding it with her left hand. She wanted to giggle again, though she knew this was a very solemn matter. Well, some people just couldn't help it.

Sabrina was the most giddy and humorous one. Outside of the horrors of Biology class, saying two thirds of her current life was spent laughing or giggling would NOT be an exaggeration.

Zach sighed loudly. In all their fussing, Magaritte and Sabrina forgot to listen to the important things. They also forgot to be serious. Solemn.

"Hilton gambled. And he lost, of course. He lost a lot, actually."

The interviewer nodded a little.

"So he asked me if I could lend him some money. I mean, we WERE good friends before." Zach bit hard on the word "WERE," as if to prove clearly to everyone that their friendship had ended. Hilton's heart still froze a little, missing a tiny beat, when he heard the word "were."

It started raining outside. There was a pitter-patter of the raindrops on bored plants. The room went silent again, for a while, without Zach's deep voice. There was only the quiet sound of the camera buzzing.

"And I said yes." Zach continued. "It was, like, $200,000. I don't know anyone else that risked such huge gambling bets."

"He took the money," said Zach." But when the time came to return it, he refused. He didn't have the money, anyway."

Ms. Meryl widened her eyes and stared at Hilton. "Why didn't you tell me? You could have asked me!" She mouthed, or sort-of-whispered the words to Hilton. At his daughter's response, Hilton bowed his head and wouldn't budge or even look at Ms. Meryl's eyes.

Zach breathed in some raspy air. He took a short but strong look at Hilton and Ms. Meryl. He continued. "And at first I let him delay. We were friends, so I allowed him the extra time."

Again. The "WERE."

"Then I grew anxious. Because the doctor just told me my mother has lung cancer. Stage 4."

Hilton was astonished. He spoke to Zach, or somewhat to himself, "You…you…could have…I didn't know about it…Should… have told…me."

Zach heard his words. Suddenly he stood up and pounded his fist on the table. His face was red under the tan. "Do you know what our mother did for us? All three of us! She brought us up through that winter in New York! It was 3°F!" Zach's eyes were red. He snarled.

The interviewer stood up now. He was taller than Sabrina had expected. About 6'3.

He spoke in a cool, indifferent voice, as if this wasn't the first time he had to deal with these scenarios. "Please take your seat, Mr.

Cochlan." Zach was surprised to hear someone actually calling him by his last name. "And control your emotions. This is an interview. Not a boxing arena. Continue with your testimony."

Zach's anger diminished a little at the interviewer's placid but cool voice. He sat down, not taking his glaring eyes off Hilton.

Hilton curled his arms and collected his bones into a ball. He literally shrunk in his seat.

"The doctors said the fee for the surgery. Was to be $500,000. I had $250,000 myself. If he DID return the $200,000 in time, at least I could have afforded a payment plan, or gotten a loan…"

The room dipped into endless silence. Zach flew his sleeve over his eyes in a quick motion, but scratched his eyes painfully.

His voice quivered. "My mother would have lived through. They said the surgery was the last hope. If they got rid of the tumor and part of the left lung lobe, the source of the cancer. But no."

His voice echoed slightly.

"She died. And I saw. Her. Die. Right. There. In the hospital. Emergency. Room. Two weeks. Before I kidnapped Hilton." The words went out like a chunky string of malice.

"It was revenge. And I also tried once, afterwards, to steal his amulet. I heard it was worth some money. But actually I don't need it anyway. Ma was already dead, huh?" He spoke bitterly with the last four words. His view skimmed over the people listening to him, but lingered on the chief of police and his sister, the policewoman. He wanted to see their thoughts.

The policewoman and older local police chief quivered a little at this. They were all siblings, the local police chief was five years older than Zach. Zach was the youngest.

The interviewer nodded. Then he spoke again. "Did you get the amulet though?"

Zach shook his head. "No. The box. It was empty. It is still a mystery to me now where it went." He raised his eyebrows and scanned over Ms. Meryl's face, Hilton's guilty face, and the young faces of the 4 little girls.

"How are these young ladies involved anyway?" He inquired with a mocking sneer. "Huh."

"They were over at my house for a Biology study group that ended early. They volunteered to help me. And they are such good researchers they were very helpful. So I welcomed it." Ms. Meryl protected the girls with the fierceness she used to shield Hilton, such was the cold tone of her voice that it gave away no sign of feeling. She realized it was an unusual dynamic.

"Cool." Zach shrugged carelessly and in a disrespectful way.

Ms. Meryl was irritated. But she kept it to herself, and later on dissolved it.

The interviewer asked. "Where is the amulet now?" The question was to every one of them.

Ms. Meryl remembered something. She said seriously but a little quietly, "I found it. It was in the local cinema, near where I teach school. It was broken, the string was cut in half too."

"That was…where... I was... abducted." Hilton, who had not spoken the whole meeting, croaked out.

"Yeah." Zach nodded.

"You cut through it. With that knife you had." Hilton directed this towards Zach. "I left it there on purpose. I hoped people would find it and save me."

Zach laughed, but it was a self-mocking laugh. "Looks like your hopes were fulfilled. What about mine? I want my mother back."

The interviewer had one more question for Zach... "Lastly. How are you related to these two people?"

"We are siblings. We share the same mother. We all knew who Hilton was." At the name "Hilton," Zach glared again.

~ ~ ~

"Wanna get some milkshakes?" Sabrina hopped out into the sweltering summer heat.

"Sure. I'll get strawberry." Dara nodded. She was hot too.

Magaritte raised her eyebrows. The enthusiastic type. That's a "yes" for sure. "You know me, right? Banana brings you through the blast." Magaritte laughed a little at her own alliteration joke. The three other girls giggled with her too.

"Rachel?" Sabrina asked.

"Of course! I'll get the chocolate one! I really fell in love with that one." Rachel kicked a loose stone on the sidewalk. They turned right abruptly and headed into the 'Coffee Creams And Cones' shop. The cool air conditioning blasted into their faces.

"Hello ma'am?" Sabina called to the middle aged woman running the counter.

"How may I help you, young ladies?"

"2 chocolate shakes, 1 banana cream shake, and 1 strawberry shake please. Don't forget to add whipped cream on top please!" Sabrina turned around and smiled at Dara. Dara smiled back.

"Sure. Actually, those are the best-sellers. You girls have got taste!"

~   ~   ~

A new day at school. Awesome, the school year was not yet over. Sabrina yawned. The case was solved and the suspense was over. Back to her own placid school life. It was fun, she had to admit, and adventurous, but nonetheless she felt nothing could be better than her mom's homemade brownies and a cup of milk.

She started off for the bus station. Her legs were sore from the adventures before, but she was in a peppy mood and nothing could deny that.

~　　　~　　　~

Oh, my God. Sabrina still trembled a little at the familiar, endless ringing of the Biology class bell. Monotonous, repetitive, and most annoying, Sabrina thought as she rolled her eyes in her head.

Back to the same old life again. She had two points of focus. She was watching Dara's head, that was bent lower than usual to study Biology problems. She was also looking at Claude and making sure his popped gum didn't reach her hair. So there she was, staring at those two people for the whole biology class, until Ms. Meryl landed a 61-point test sheet on her desk.

"Um-mm." Ms. Meryl raised her eyebrows and gave that You-should-start-doing-some-work-little-lady look. Sabrina shivered a little as Ms. Meryl gave her the Ghost-looks. Somehow, though, they weren't as spine-chilling or spooky as before. Hmm. Maybe Ms. Meryl had gotten more gentle. Sabrina shook the idea out of her red, frizzy hair as Ms. Meryl accurately landed a stack of practice papers on her desk. Well. She had some work to do, if that didn't tire her out.

Claude wasn't chewing gum, so therefore Sabrina's hair was safe. Alright. No more sticky painted gum-in-hair, or detention. She stared at Claude's slightly wiggling mouth.

Is that…wait...what is Claude chewing…? Oh no. It's gum.

THE END

Dora is a 12-year-old 6th grader and loves writing. She is a total bookworm! (Hmm…favorite book? Little Women, of course!) Currently living in Hangzhou, China, she has many hobbies like reading, art, and playing the piano. She got the inspiration of this book from a detective scenario they played in class, and she was intrigued by it. She loved suspense! (And added LOTS in her story that she hoped you enjoyed…) She got home and started working feverishly on this little book for a year. In the process there were many obstacles, like facing writer's block, but she was able to finish it at the end. (Not exactly the easiest thing in the world)